Mad Duke March

THE RAKE REVIEW
BOOK THREE

SADIE BOSQUE

First edition

Editing by Tracy Liebchen

Cover art by Dar Albert

Series logo by Sadie Bosque

 Created with Vellum

To fighting our demons.

Acknowledgement

Thanks to all the Brazen Belles authors for creating a super supportive community that is easy and fun to work with.

Thanks to all the Brazen Belles readers for your love, encouragement, and for participating in our authors' journey.

If you don't know what I'm talking about, be sure to join The Brazen Belles Facebook Group! You'll get to hang out with all your favorite Rake Review authors and a community of amazing historical romance fans.

Content Note

This work of fiction contains adult content, strong language, bullying, excessive use of alcohol, parental estrangement, pregnancy, CPTSD, and other content that might be triggering to some.

Reader discretion is advised.

Prologue

Ireland
September 1819

This place reeked of anguish, despair, and misery.

Neither the warm glow cast by the towering, candle-filled chandelier nor the light filtering through the tall windows could drive away the chill that permeated anyone daring to step inside the house. For despite its beauty and luxury, darkness had taken up residence within these walls.

Alexander Blackwood, the new Duke of Tyrone, paused at the base of the grand staircase of his ancestral home.

The air hung heavy with the scent of aged wooden floors, flickering candles, and ancient oil paintings.

Bile rose in his throat, though it had nothing to do with the smell. It was the place itself.

He unhurriedly ascended the steps, his gloved fingers gliding over the mahogany banister, each step accompanied by the creak of the stairs.

His stomach twisted as he traversed the first-floor corridor. Everything was as he remembered it—the disapproving gazes of previous dukes followed him from the faded tapestries, the clicks of his heels were muted by the crimson Turkish carpet, and the benches between doors invited him to sit and contemplate what trouble he had gotten himself into before entering the lion's den.

A little boy—an apparition—appeared before his eyes, if only for a moment. There he was, sitting on that bench, his hands clasped close to his stomach as he rocked back and forth, mumbling—no, praying—to himself.

As the vision disappeared, he opened the door to his father's study and peered inside.

The desk stood in the middle of the room, its polished surface ready for the master to come in and resume his work. Two wing-back chairs flanked an empty hearth, a chess game arranged on a little table between them as if someone was about to sit down and play.

"Look at me when I talk to you!" The voice reverberated through his mind, causing him to shudder. *"You useless little idiot! You can't do anything right!"*

The sound of clattering chess pieces across the floor followed as the chessboard flew toward him. He raised his arms instinctively, only to realize that he was shielding himself from his memories. His breathing labored, he shook his head before storming out of the room.

Taking two steps at a time, he climbed to the second floor and stalked toward the most familiar room. He pushed the door open, and his entire body went rigid.

Nothing had changed there either.

It was as if he'd never left.

A sturdy oak four-poster bed stood in the center, with a faded green coverlet on top. A desk nestled in the corner, flanked by book-filled shelves.

Even his little trunk still stood by the window.

The boy's apparition reappeared, perched on the trunk, gazing out the window, a glimmer of hope smoldering within.

"She is not coming back, you useless loiter-sack! And it's all because of you," the slurred ghostly voice of his father echoed, followed by a string of hurtful insults, until eventually, the duke would express his rage by replacing words with objects hurled through the air, aimed at his son's head. Soon his fists and cane would join the list of things crashing into his son's shaking body.

"Tyrone!"

He tensed before realizing this wasn't a memory. It was his ginger-haired friend, the Earl of Sutton, calling him from the other end of the corridor.

Will I ever get used to being addressed by this wretched title?

It had been two months since he inherited the dukedom, but it still rang hollow to his ears. No, it struck fear and loathing into his heart.

Sutton approached him, pausing only a few paces away. "What do you want to do now?"

Throwing one last glance at his former room, his gaze lingered at the little trunk by the window that tugged at his heart. "Sell everything valuable," he said, before turning away from the room and walking resolutely away. "Burn the rest."

He paused on the staircase landing overlooking the hall. "And then we shall have a drink."

Chapter One

London
March 1820

"Fire it up, Chaos," Tyrone said and took a large swig of whisky, the liquid burning its path through his throat as he leaned against the giant, black-lacquered carriage and glanced down at the busy street.

People bustled about, hurrying in and out of the Petticoat Lane market, while street vendors called out their wares. Amidst the cacophony, the sounds of repairs going on in the street lingered in the air, the pungent scent of fresh paint wafted from buckets, and the clatter of ladders lined up by the roadside filled the scene.

Mr. Charles Thomas Hunter, a man his friends and subsequently all of England called Chaos, walked up to the firebox in the huge, metallic boiler and ignited the fuel.

Chaos was a man of few words but many interests. With his dark brown unruly hair, wild, fiery gaze, and rumpled cravat, he should have been the one to be dubbed the Madman of London, or at the very least the Mad Man of Science.

Somehow, the honor of getting the Mad moniker had fallen to Tyrone. Why? That would forever remain a mystery to him.

"I don't think this is the best place to test this monster," Sutton said. "The street is filled with people."

"Therein lies the challenge," Tyrone replied and took another swig of burning liquid. His mind now cleared, the color had returned all around him, the sounds of the busy street bothering him less than before. "Can an experimental steam carriage make it past the busy street without incident and without causing much distress?"

"I wager it can't," Tyrone's other friend, Lucien Drake, chimed in. There were two or three other gentlemen with them, but Tyrone did not remember their names. They were young, drunk, and enthusiastic about the experiment. That was all Tyrone needed to know.

"Then we shall make the papers!" Tyrone insisted. "And Chaos's new invention will get the due it deserves."

"Or we shall spend the night in the gaol," Sutton noted darkly.

Tyrone let out a bark of laughter. "I am a duke. Besides, this, by far, is the least outrageous thing I have done in my life, and I have always come away unscathed."

Perhaps, *that's* why he was called the Mad Duke.

Tyrone loved testing the limits of any endeavor, including, but not limited to, his tolerance for alcohol and other people's reactions to unhinged behavior. He was always placing—and winning—the most audacious wagers and coming up with the most damning escapades.

He barely finished the sentence when, as if summoned from the ether by Sutton's words or Tyrone's own daring, two constables appeared before them.

"Pardon me, m'lords, but you can't be testing your machine here!" one of them yelled over the sounds of the engine. "You can't be driving that thing on the public roads."

Tyrone laughed. "Do you not know who I am, sir? I'll not be told where I can and cannot drive my own carriage! Or any carriage, for that matter."

"We do know who you are, sir," the second constable, the older of the two, with a few gray hairs peeking out from under his hat and a rounded belly under his coat, insisted. "This isn't the first time you've attempted this feat. And unless you received proper authorization for that beast of a machine, it is not allowed to be out on the streets!"

"This is merely a trial run," Lucien said calmly, patting the man on his shoulder and smoothly maneuvering both constables away from the noise. "Certainly two men of the law won't stand in the way of progress?"

He was trying to distract them. Tyrone looked around and a fabulous idea entered his mind.

"On my signal start the machine," he told Chaos and walked away.

"What signal?" Chaos shouted over the noise of the engine, but Tyrone just smirked.

The younger constable shook his head. "Apologies, milords. Rules are rules. As long as that carriage hasn't got proper patents or permissions, we cannot allow it on the streets."

Tyrone emptied his flask, shaking the last drop into his mouth. Then he picked up a bucket of red paint and a brush and cocked his head toward his friends. "Lucien needs our help distracting the constables. Let's lend him a hand, shall we?"

With that, he proceeded to paint the doors and signs of the houses red. The other gentlemen followed his cue, knocking off flowerpots, paint buckets, and otherwise sowing chaos.

Constables, forgetting about the steam-carriage, ran after Tyrone and his friends, trying unsuccessfully to stop them.

Just then, Chaos pulled the lever, and the carriage rattled toward them.

"See here!" the older constable yelled, waving in a feeble

attempt to stop the barreling carriage. "You stop this instant or arrests shall be made!"

"Arrests!" Tyrone scoffed. "We haven't done anything wrong. It's all in the name of science."

He bellowed in laughter and stepped aside, watching the carriage pick up speed, careening recklessly down the road as people leapt aside. The gentlemen whooped and hollered in triumph over the sputtering engine.

So much for the unpatented vehicle causing panic. Everything was going well!

Just then, a young maiden—not looking where she was going —stepped into the paint Tyrone had spilled onto the street, reeled in shock, and swayed right onto the carriage's path.

It was the happiest day of her life.

Emily Fitzwilliam was bursting with excitement as she hurried toward Petticoat Lane with a skip in her step, ready to buy the silk and lace necessary to fix her and her sisters' gowns. After all, she was getting married soon!

The image of Bernard on his knees before her, reciting a line of poetry he'd written as he asked for her hand in marriage floated through her mind. He was such a romantic.

She clasped her hands before her chest, not caring that people looked strangely her way.

It didn't matter what was happening around her.

The street was dirty and noisy. The scent of paint from the ongoing street repairs made her nauseous. A few feet away, a few gentlemen argued with the constables next to a large carriage with a metal box on top, emanating steam. Well-dressed ladies and gentlemen passed through the street to get to or from the Petticoat Lane market, giving her disapproving side glances. A few boys ran around looking to pick those well-to-do ladies and gentlemen's pockets. But it might as well have been an enchanting forest with whistling songbirds.

Nothing could ruin Emily's mood.

Bernard—the man she had been in love with since she was fifteen—had finally proposed to her! Soon, she would have a family of her own, while at the same time saving her mother and siblings from poverty.

As much as she loved Bernard, she could not help but take into consideration the fact that marrying a well-to-do viscount's third son would help find suitors for her sisters and possibly even help afford school for her little brother Reggie!

She twirled in glee, her arms stretched wide at her sides, her reticule dangling from her fingers.

Plop!

Emily came to a halt, before slowly prying her foot from a red, sticky liquid.

What is that?

Wrinkling her nose from the pungent smell, she stumbled backward. It was paint! She had stepped into bright red paint, successfully ruining her favorite slippers.

Gasps and shouts rose around her, forcing Emily to look up only to see a gigantic, monstrous carriage accelerating her way.

Emily froze in horror, helplessly watching as the carriage barreled toward her.

Is it a carriage? If it is, then where are the horses?

This ridiculous thought would have been her last if it wasn't for the strong, steel-like arms encircling her waist, gripping her close to a hard, warm body and propelling her out of the way.

The world turned and tumbled as if in a whirlwind. Everything flickered before Emily's eyes, and then... nothing.

For a moment, the world went black and a light buzz in her ears obscured all other sounds. Emily opened her eyes and had to blink a few times before she was able to recognize the gray London sky.

Her head vibrated with a vicious headache, and she couldn't take in a full breath. Why was it difficult to breathe?

Emily tried to move her limbs before finally realizing what restricted her breathing and movements—the large, warm body of a very heavy male who was lying on top of her!

She tried to turn her head, but his hair was in her face, tickling her nose and wiggling its way into her mouth.

Panic gripped her tightly from the inside. She flailed her arms, trying to shake the gentleman off her.

It seemed to work as the stranger raised his face just enough to look into her eyes.

"Who are ye?" he slurred terribly as the smell of alcohol hit her face.

The strange man stared at her with a dazed look in his eyes. Despite his pitch-black hair with not even a hint of silver, the unkempt beard on his face made him look sixty years old.

She wriggled, hoping to dislodge the man from her. "Please, remove yourself from my body."

"I am not in yer body." On top of a drunken slur, the man had the hint of an Irish brogue.

Her nose scrunched and bile rose to her throat. *Splendid!* The only thing she needed now was to cast up her accounts. That ought to help with the situation.

He tried moving again, but his hands were underneath her body, while he pinned her down to the ground with his weight, making it impossible for either of them to get up.

The man shifted to raise his torso, but the attempt proved unsuccessful, and he collapsed against her chest once more.

"Why are ye still on top of me?" he slurred, his unpleasant breath hitting her face.

Her face burning, Emily pushed at his chest. "*You* are the one on top of *me*!"

"Impossible," the man mumbled by her ear. "Yer arse is on my hands."

He flexed his hands, to prove his point, squeezing her buttocks.

Emily gasped. "How dare you! Get off me, immediately!"

He was lying indecently in the cradle of her thighs, and if that wasn't bad enough, her skirts hiked up her knees.

"Are they copulating?" A horrified, loud cry sounded from the crowd forming around them.

"In public?"

"Look away, darling!" someone else called.

"Hold on a moment," the man murmured, before grasping her tighter, and rolling over until she was the one on top of him.

Emily pushed off his shoulders and tried to move away, only to be held back, by the stranger's hands, still holding on to her rump. She sat up, still on top of him, and wriggled, trying to get away, shaking in humiliated horror.

The sounds of gasps and hushed whispers intensified as the crowd continued their speculation of what was going on.

"I said, hold on a moment," the man growled.

"I am straddling you like a gelding in front of the entire world. Please, forgive me for not being patient!" Emily cried.

"If you were to compare me to a horse, I'd prefer a stallion, if you don't mind," he answered gravely. "Ah, there it is!" He finally let go of her bottom, pulling his hands out of his gloves. "The gloves were stuck to your gown. Now, off you go."

She slid sideways onto the pavement, her hands still shaking, while the man stood ungracefully and tugged on his coat repeatedly, before staggering away.

A hand appeared before her—a masculine, large hand enclosed in a fine white silk glove. Emily raised her head and was met by an angel with glinting blue eyes and golden-red hair.

Emily took his hand without thinking and was quickly helped to her feet.

"Ow!" Before Emily was able to collect her wits, a blinding pain accosted her ankle. She almost fell—would have fallen—if not for the ginger-haired stranger's steady arms. "Apologies, I think my ankle is twisted." To her immense horror, her voice came out shaky and her eyes filled with tears.

"No need to worry," he said softly in a soothing baritone. He was the opposite of the man who had crushed her just a moment ago. Young, gorgeous, polite. "Let me escort you to my carriage."

"No, I can't—" Emily moved her head, only to wince from the piercing headache that was gone as quickly as it came. When she looked around, she finally saw the gathering crowd around them.

Oh, heavens!

Emily glanced down at herself and was horrified at the state of her clothing. Her skirt was ripped, a couple of gloves were stuck to her derriere, and patches of red paint were all over her gown.

She raised her hand to her head and realized that not only was her hair tumbling out of her coiffure, but a part of it was covered by paint, too!

"You can't walk. And I can't leave you here. So, we'll need to compromise. Either I carry you to your house in my arms, or you take my carriage."

Emily blinked, her throat burning as a huge boulder stuck inside it. But she looked down at her torn, dirty gown that had streaks of red paint on it and realized that she was not going to get home on foot. At least, not with her dignity intact.

Dignity?

Emily raised her head and looked at the crowd of onlookers still whispering about, their heads bowed toward each other.

Her dignity was thrown to the ground just as she had been a moment ago. Unlike her, her dignity had also been stomped on. And then cold sweat covered her from head to toe as another realization hit her. She looked at her hands, her breathing growing shallow. "My reticule!"

"Do not worry about the damage done by the paint," the

ginger-haired angel said softly. "We'll be certain to rectify any damage."

"No." Emily shook her head in distress. "My reticule, it's gone!" And all the money was gone with it.

She looked around the street and studied the paint-caked ground. No use. The reticule was nowhere to be found.

"I can ask my men to comb the entire street," the ginger-haired stranger offered, concern shining in his eyes.

Emily nodded absently and swallowed the lump in her throat. "Thank you." She whipped around to see young street boys disappearing around the corner. Pick-pockets. Most likely, her reticule was already in their skillful hands.

"Good." The gentleman took her hand and, ignoring her protest, placed it in the crook of his arm, letting her lean on him as she half walked-half hopped alongside him.

Emily's mind reeled as she surveyed the chaos around the street. The red paint was strewn about the road and even adorned some of the buildings. A carriage with no horses steamed at the end of the street, crashed into a pole. A few gentlemen surrounded the constables, shouting and waving their hands.

But she couldn't care less about any of it as she tried to reconcile with the fact that the money was gone and her clothing was ruined. More importantly, she was ruined!

Cold sweat ran down her back again, and she hid her face from the onlookers. Her cheeks burned in shame and her mind refused to cooperate and think of anything that would help her get out of this situation with her life not in ruins.

Her breaths came out in short gulps, panic screaming in her mind.

"Are you unwell? Miss... Miss?" The words came as if from far away. The angel beside her had stopped and looked into her eyes with a great deal of worry.

"Miss Fitzwilliam," Emily supplied her name. "Miss Emily Fitzwilliam."

She clamped her lips shut and looked around the street at the people still ogling her and whispering behind their fans.

She shouldn't have said her name. Someone could have heard. It was the polite thing to do. But now people knew who she was.

Her family could be ruined by this.

Oh, God, Oh, God, Oh, God!

"Breathe," the ginger-haired stranger said calmly. "Everything will be just fine. Come with me."

He led her away, and she walked beside him on legs that felt as sturdy as wool, with no other choice but to obey his instructions.

They reached a shiny black-lacquered carriage at that time and a young footman in gorgeous green livery opened the carriage door and lowered the step.

Emily peeked at the plush velvet upholstery, her gaze glassy. "I shall cover the interior with paint," she said in a defeated voice.

The gentleman beside her nodded to his footman, and he quickly pulled out a worn quilt from under the bench. He spread it over the seat, before helping Emily inside.

"It was a pleasure to meet you, Miss Emily Fitzwilliam." The gentleman bowed low. "Please, take my card. If there are any unfortunate repercussions for you from this incident, *any repercussions whatsoever,* please, do not hesitate to contact me."

He closed the door and only then did Emily realize that he hadn't even introduced himself. She twirled the card in her fingers before reading his name.

The Earl of Sutton.

Chapter Two

"Do not wince, Em!" Harriet, Emily's younger sister, pleaded to no avail as Emily's entire body scrunched up in fear, regret, and sorrow. "I shall cut off more than necessary if you keep doing that!"

"Oh, very well!" Emily screeched. She stilled in the chair, staring at the wall of the sisters' bedroom in the little cottage they'd rented for the duration of their stay in London. "But do be quick about it!"

"If I am quick about it, it shall be all wrong!" Harriet snapped back. As the second oldest sibling, she had trimmed Emily's hair before. But this was different.

"It won't be right no matter what you do," Emily whimpered in defeat and squeezed her eyes shut. Her breath caught as she heard a crunching sound followed by a resounding snip. Emily stilled, not moving a muscle, not even breathing as her sister continued cutting her hair.

Crunch. Snip. Crunch. Snip.

Tears rolled down Emily's cheeks, but she refused to make a sound.

And then the gentle, "All done."

With shaking fingers, Emily raised a small mirror from her lap. She stared at it for a long moment not recognizing the person staring back. She quickly looked away from her red and puffy eyes toward the rough edges of her now short hair and an involuntary sob tore from her mouth. "I look hideous!"

Emily rarely lost her composure in front of her siblings. She needed to be strong for them. She needed to set a good example and be the one reassuring them.

But so many things had gone wrong in one morning that she had no capacity to hold all of that inside.

Hair, clothes, humiliation, ruination. Poverty!

Since the hair was the last straw that broke Emily's composure, her hair would be the one thing she complained about.

Harriet's skirts rustled as she took a step back. Her voice was small, hollow even. "I did my best."

Tears fell freely, burning their path along Emily's cheeks. "How am I supposed to get married looking like this?" *Will I even get a chance to get married at all after this?*

Silence.

Emily turned to look at Harriet, only to see her wringing her hands, her lower lip protruding and quivering, her dark brown eyes liquid, making her look as vulnerable and hurt as when Emily had chastised her when she was little. She was seventeen—an adult. But to Emily, she would always be a little child.

"I am sorry, Harry. I am not upset with you." Emily wanted nothing more than to soothe her little sister. However, she was too dismayed to make a real effort, her emotions too raw to switch from hurt and bitterness to comfort and reassurance. She loved Harry, and it pained to see her hurt, but Harry's beautiful chestnut hair tumbling down her shoulders only salted the wounds in her soul.

She raised the mirror back to her face and studied her brown locks of hair haphazardly pointing this way and that. "You did... well." She swallowed. Her once long golden-brown locks, the ones she brushed every night and took pride in their glow in the light of candles, were now destroyed. In their place was something that looked disturbingly like a pile of hay. And Emily herself resembled a homeless mutt.

"I can't marry Bernard like this!" Emily exclaimed as she hurled the mirror onto the bed. What she really meant was that Bernard was not going to marry her like that. He loved her golden-brown tresses and told her constantly they were her best feature.

Emily had never been beautiful. Not the way her sisters were. And deep in her heart, she liked that there was something about her that Bernard found exceptional.

"Finally, some good news," Sophie said from behind her.

Emily turned toward her, heat creeping up her face. "Pardon me?"

"Sophie, not now!" Harriet tried to shoo their youngest sister away, but Sophie evaded her skillfully and danced farther into the room.

"It doesn't look that bad," she said, although her scrunched-up face proved her words a lie. She glanced from the locks on the floor back to Emily's face before turning to Harriet. "Did you have to cut it this short?"

"I did my best." Harry threw up her hands. "And you just said it didn't look that bad!"

"It does not!" Sophie insisted, her freckled nose still wrinkled. "But it would look better longer."

"If I could make it longer, why would I have cut it this short?" Harry's voice trembled and her hands shook as she started collecting the hair off the floor.

"Oh, God, Harry, are you crying?" Sophie scoffed. "You are not the one marrying Bernard."

"Sophie!" Harry exclaimed, in horror, but Emily couldn't scrounge up an ounce of outrage anymore. She felt defeated. There was too much distress in her heart to argue.

Both her sisters harbored an open dislike of her fiancé. It wasn't his fault, really. Bernard's younger sister was Emily's age, and he didn't know how to interact with anyone younger. So, he either treated them as babies or avoided them altogether.

But the fact that Harry was now trying to silence Sophie instead of supporting her just underlined how terrible Emily must have looked.

"I think you look quite handsome," Reggie said as he strode inside the room. At eleven years old, he was the youngest sibling.

"Thank you," Emily said with a tender smile.

"Now your hair is shorter than mine!" he said proudly, immediately wiping the smile off Emily's face. He wasn't wrong.

"Reggie, go back to your studies," Sophie admonished.

"But I am already done!"

As the pair continued to bicker, Harry sat beside Emily and took her hand. "Perhaps we can buy you a beautiful wig."

Emily just sniffed. A quality wig would cost a fortune. And the Fitzwilliam family didn't own a fortune. Not to mention that Emily had managed to lose the only money they had for accessories along with her dignity and her hair this morning. Their dire financial situation was one of the few reasons why Emily had packed up her family and came to London to force—no, force was too strong a word—*compel* Bernard to honor his promise and propose to her. Another one of the reasons was even more dire...

She didn't want to even think about that now. Besides, she wasn't certain that reason even existed. There were more pressing matters at the moment. Such as going to Bernard and telling him about what had transpired that morning, hoping that his family wouldn't care about her hair ruining the ceremony and that the marriage would proceed as planned. Hoping, too, that the rumors about this morning's unfortunate incident hadn't reached his ears yet, because if they had, it could be distorted as much as cruel society wanted.

She would hate to ruin his honor by association if vicious

rumors circulated. However, there was no other choice. He either married her, ruined reputation and all, or her family would be ruined even more.

There was a possibility that nobody had recognized her as the one involved in the incident this morning. She had never made a debut. Nobody truly knew who she was.

But Petticoat Lane had been crowded, and many people could have overheard as she introduced herself to the Earl of Sutton. And the earl himself, or one of his friends, could be the ones to spread the rumors, exaggerating the details. Emily was not privy to the ways of the *ton*, but in her little village, if a person sneezed, people would say that they had caused a wind storm. If London gossip spread anything similar to their village ways, she feared what the rumors would say about her accident.

She had been lying on her back, her ankles bared, with a man on top of her! No matter how innocent the situation, it wouldn't seem that way to the onlookers.

Not every man would be able to look past such rumors. Bernard would, though. He would protect her and her family.

Now, more than ever, she had to believe in that.

"Let go of me!" Reggie shoved his sister, and Sophie barreled after him with a gasp.

"Enough!" their mother called from the threshold and everyone's heads snapped back to look at her.

Their mother stood there, with her arm on the door jamb, her eyes puffy, her hair let down and gently laying against her shoulders.

"Mother!" Emily attempted to stand but immediately sat back on her chair with a wince as a piercing pain shot through her ankle. "Did we wake you?"

Her mother threw her a weak smile before turning her stern gaze to her other siblings. "Let your sister rest now. I think you've done enough."

"We weren't doing anything." Sophie shrugged but filed out

of the room, following her siblings under her mother's compelling gaze.

Their mother let out a breath of relief when all of them turned the corner and continued their bickering on the way down the stairs. Then she turned her piercing gaze to Emily, and Emily hid her eyes. She knew that one look from her mother could make her confess all her sins.

"I am glad to see you on your feet. Your migraine is gone, then?" Emily asked, crimping the skirt of her gown.

Her mother hesitated. "I feel well enough to check on my daughter."

Tears formed in the back of Emily's eyes, and she was unable to face her mother lest those tears trickle down her cheeks and worry her.

Her mother walked up to Emily's bed and sat beside her. Warm fingers touched Emily's chin prompting her to meet her mother's kind eyes. And that was all it took for Emily to break down. "I lost the money, Mama," she whispered before tears trailed down her cheeks. She hadn't told her siblings that, only that she was tackled and badly hurt. It wasn't their cross to bear. But she couldn't keep anything from her mother. She fisted her hands so hard that her palms hurt. "I am so sorry and so ashamed. But I ruined everything!"

Emily was the one responsible for the finances in their household. She was the one to buy food and keep the family clothed; she was even the one to pay their only servant. All their guardian did was distribute their allowance. He didn't care about the family, and neither did he care about their tiny parcel of land. He was much more likely to squander everything away before Reggie reached his majority.

But today, Emily realized she'd made substantial mistakes, too. She had already spent a significant amount of the family's money on this trip to London. Her family in tow, she'd risked it all in the hope of persuading Bernard to marry her. But she'd always been careful and she never carried large amounts of money with her.

Until this morning.

She needed money to purchase fabric, order outfits for the entire family, and buy accessories and shoes so they would look respectable in front of Bernard's family and the wedding guests. She didn't know how much she'd need to spend, so she'd taken almost all of it, only leaving behind enough for a rainy day.

A huge mistake.

Now it was all gone. And Emily would likely have to marry Bernard in old rags, not to mention her hair. More pressingly, her mother and siblings' appearance would be reduced to shambles as well.

Her mother's eyes turned liquid before she embraced Emily and patted her head. "Oh, my poor child."

Emily let out a wretched sob as she sank deeper into her mother's arms. "I was humiliated, hurt... I ruined my clothing, my hair, and lost all the money." Her voice grew hoarse, and she sniffed every so often, her words muffled against her mother's frock.

"Don't cry, child," her mother said, her fingers weaving through Emily's short hair. "Everything will turn out well."

Emily could handle almost anything. She would be fine with scolding, and she would stand strong through recriminations and accusations. Because ultimately, she deserved it all.

But her mother's kindness was something that melted her soul.

Emily had to be brave and strong for her entire family ever since her father's death five years ago. Her mother was sickly often. She did as much as she could around the household when she felt better, but all the financial burdens had fallen onto Emily's fragile shoulders.

Moments like this, however, were when Emily remembered why she was still standing, why she was able to bear it all. Because no matter what, she had her mother at her side. A mother who always supported her, loved her, and comforted her. A mother who never judged her, even when she should have.

Emily raised her head and wiped her tears, her voice shaking as she said, "Yes, it will. Because I'll fix it. I'll go to Bernard, explain everything, and hope that wagging tongues haven't turned him against me yet."

Her mother shook her head, cupping Emily's cheek tenderly, and wiping away the tears with her thumb. "If he truly loves you, nothing anybody says will matter to him. You shouldn't worry."

"But I have failed him, Mama. I shall come to his home in rags, with nothing to bring to the table but a few mouths to feed and a scandal. I won't even have a decent wedding gown."

Her mother patted her cheek lovingly. "Yes, my darling. You shall." She gently opened the palm of her other hand and nudged it toward Emily. There nestled a simple silver wedding band with *Amelia*, her mother's name, inscribed on the inside. Her mother's wedding band. "We can take it to the pawnbroker tomorrow. A simple silver band won't fetch much, but it should be enough to buy lace and silk. We won't be able to purchase new clothing, but I can fix your favorite gown for your wedding."

Emily's eyes widened. "You want me to sell your wedding band?"

Her mother just shrugged, her lips pursed, her features unreadable. "It's just a ring, darling."

"It is not! It is the band Papa put on your finger when you wed. It is the last thing you have of him. As you said, it won't fetch much, and it will be lost forever!"

"It is not the last thing I have of him, darling," her mother said softly. "You and your siblings are the first, the last, and the most important things your father gave me. And he wouldn't want you to suffer just so we could keep the ring in the family. He loved you more than that ring. And so do I." She took Emily's hands in hers and squeezed. "Now, you can feel pity for your situation for a little while, that's quite fine. I will be right here to comfort you. But once you're done, we can sell that ring, use that money to fix your gown, and go to Bernard to make arrangements for your upcoming nuptials."

Tears glistened in Emily's eyes. "But, Mother—"

"No buts, darling. I have had the most wonderful marriage anyone could have ever had. And if this ring helps you get your turn... I couldn't have asked for more."

Emily wiped her tears and licked her dry and puffy lips. She would never sell her mother's ring. She would marry wearing rags before she would part with a symbol of the eternal love her mother had for her father. But the fact that her mother was willing to part with it just to make life easier for Emily meant a lot to her. "Thank you, Mama."

"Of course, my child." She caressed Emily's hair. "Sometimes I think you forget that *I* am the mother, not you. I am the one who is supposed to take care of you. And I shall always be by your side."

Emily relaxed against her mother's soft shoulder and inhaled the familiar scent of lavender, feeling safe again.

"Now that I see your mood has brightened," her mother said, "I think you're ready to read this missive." She pulled out an envelope from the pocket of her skirt and handed it to Emily.

"What is it?" Emily asked as she took it with trembling fingers before quickly drying her tears with the sleeves of her gown.

Her mother stood and dusted her skirts. "It's a letter from Bernard. It came just a few minutes ago. I shall leave you to read it on your own time. But call me if you need anything." With a quick smile, her mother turned away and left the room.

Emily hastily opened the letter, her heart racing in her chest as if she'd run for miles. Her hands shook as her gaze ran down the lines of the missive.

. . .

Dearest Emily,

My heart is heavy as an anvil as I commit these words to paper. Rumors, like venomous serpents, have slithered their way to my ears, carrying tales of your entanglement with the Duke of Tyrone, poisoning the well of love in my soul.

What? Emily couldn't believe her eyes. Cold sweat covered her body as she skimmed through the rest of the letter, catching glimpses of sentences that shattered her heart.

Your betrayal has torn at the very essence of my being...

The sweet melodies of your promises now ring hollow...

I had never fathomed the depths of anguish that I could plunge into so profoundly...

I can never be certain of your sincerity. I shall forever doubt whether you carry the fruit of our love...

I find no other solution but to sever our ties—

Emily closed her eyes, taking in loud gasps of air. Hot flashes ran through her body, causing her palms and other random patches of her body to perspire.

This must be a nightmare. She swallowed, before rereading the letter from start to finish, calmer now, not missing a single word. Then she read it again. And again. Until every word was engraved in her mind.

No matter how many times she reread it, the message it carried was the same.

Bernard had heard about the rumors and was breaking off their betrothal.

Not only did the coward do it via the letter, but he had the gall to make himself a victim!

How could he have so little trust in her?

How could he have broken off the betrothal without seeing her, speaking to her, and hearing her side of the story?

Her fingers curled and crushed the letter in her fist, but it might as well have been her heart.

Bernard was not the man she thought he was.

But he was still the man who could save her.

Chapter Three

Emily got up early in the morning. Earlier than usual. She wasn't able to fall asleep anyway. What was the point of lying in bed?

She tossed and turned, her mind racing, coming up with ways to save her reputation. Only one conclusion came to mind. She needed to see Bernard, talk to him, and convince him to marry her still.

She was still angry at him; that hadn't changed. But the more she thought about it, the more certain she was that the letter was not Bernard's idea.

His parents had never been fond of Emily. This was the main reason why Bernard hadn't proposed earlier. And now, with the scandal looming over Emily's head, they, no doubt, had taken the opportunity to poison Bernard's mind.

It wasn't lost on Emily that he still had given up on her so easily. That he'd written those hurtful words without giving a chance for Emily to explain.

She had loved him since she was fifteen years old. She would never have broken off any association with him just because of a little scandal. Her emotions oscillated between betrayal, frustration, anger, and despair. But she couldn't concentrate on that now. She couldn't let her emotions cloud her judgment.

Yes, he was a coward.

But he was the coward who could still save her and her family.

She would cry and wail, and kick Bernard in the shins, but *after* the wedding. Right now, she needed to see him. See him and beg him to take her back.

And she needed to do it by herself. She couldn't let her mother be humiliated by the unfair treatment at the O'Malley house. Because as much as she believed in the goodness deep inside Bernard, she couldn't say the same about his parents.

Emily donned her most beautiful gown, her white silk slippers, and a blue Spencer jacket that she only wore on special occasions. She stared at her paint-ruined clothing for a long moment before rummaging through the pockets and collecting the card with the Earl of Sutton's name and address on it.

He'd said if there were any repercussions from the incident to come calling. She doubted he would be able to help her, but she pocketed the card all the same.

She hoped the journey to the O'Malleys' house would give her time to school her features, cool her anger, and temper her frustrations as well as give her the opportunity to come up with something better to say than "You owe me a minute of your time, you rotten scoundrel, as you promised to marry me since the day of my fifteenth birthday!"

But she underestimated her anger. When she stepped onto the O'Malleys' doorstep, she was still seething.

She was not able to let out her frustrations on anyone, however, because the butler insisted that no one was home, although Emily saw someone peeking out of the windows a few times.

Cowards. All of them.

Well, if they wanted to distance themselves from scandal, Emily would make certain to stay as close to them as possible. It wasn't as if Emily had anywhere else to go. It wasn't as if Emily could even walk far with her aching ankle. So, she sat right there on the doorstep, her elbows on her knees, her chin propped in her hands, refusing to leave even when the butler came out to shoo her away.

She refused to move even when minutes ruthlessly ticked the day away. And even after the sky opened up and rained down upon her.

Bernard's laughing face played before her eyes, the memory as fresh as if it had been yesterday.

They had been perched on a log, near a tranquil stream, their hair tousled by the warm, gentle breeze. As Emily's unruly locks had danced in her face, Bernard had reached out, brushing them aside, his lips graced by a radiant smile.

"I shall marry you someday, Emily Fitzwilliam," he had *declared with unwavering certainty. "You'll see."*

And she had believed him wholeheartedly, with every fiber of her being.

Idiot.

Emily brushed the wet, short locks away from her face and shivered, soaked to her bones and extremely cold when the door opened once more and someone tentatively stepped out of the house.

Bernard?

Emily raised her head, but her excitement dimmed as she saw Astrid, Bernard's younger sister instead.

Emily watched Astrid, her friend of many years, and wondered if she would twist the knife in her heart that Bernard had left there.

Astrid let out a sigh and gingerly sat next to Emily, dragging the silk skirt of her gown along the wet, dirty step.

"I am sorry about everything that happened," she said simply.

Emily blinked, not certain what her reply should be. "Thank you," she mustered through her dry and scratchy throat.

"The rumors..." Astrid paused. "Mother said even the servants were talking."

Emily blinked away the rain. "About me?"

Astrid nodded with a grimace. "About your *incident* with the duke."

"The rumors are lies; you must convince your brother." Emily took Astrid by her shoulders in desperation. "I was nearly run down by a carriage and the duke saved me, knocking me onto the ground. I had never met him before, surely Bernard knows that. He knows me! If I just talked to him and told him the truth—"

Astrid covered her hands and squeezed, before gently moving them away from her shoulders. "The truth is... inconsequential. The rumors are all that matters. My parents will never accept you. They pressured Bernie to sever his associations with you, threatening to cut him off."

Emily's brow creased in confusion. She pulled back her arms, curling her fingers into fists on her lap. "He doesn't need their money. He has a well-respected job. If that is not enough, I can work, too! If he marries me, that would counter all the rumors and we can weather it all. But my ruination affects my family, my siblings!" *My future.*

Astrid grimaced and looked away. "He is not going to marry you."

Emily's lower lip trembled, and she had to bite it to keep from crying. Astrid's words were so final they broke Emily's heart.

She stared at Astrid with a glassy gaze while in her heart she wanted to scream and wail, and even shake Astrid until she took her words back.

Bernard loved her. She knew he loved her. He was probably hurting and didn't mean anything he'd said. He was going to look past the ugly rumors and accept the person he loved. Astrid had just misunderstood him, surely.

But Astrid spoke again, softer now. "After he sent the farewell note to you, he immediately sent flowers to Miss Bertha

Godfrey." She cleared her throat and lowered her voice once more. "He is going to see her today. He is going to start courting her."

Astrid might as well have pulled out the knife with Emily's heart still attached to it.

Miss Bertha Godfrey. She'd heard that name from Bernard before. A respectable, agreeable young woman. A baron's niece with a sizable dowry.

The sharp pain in Emily's chest, the terrible headache, and the lack of oxygen in her lungs rendered her speechless. Astrid continued speaking, but Emily didn't hear her anymore.

What am I to do?

Emily dreaded going back home and telling her family that all was indeed lost. And that there was no way for her to fix that.

She had promised her family a better life. She had promised her sisters better prospects in marriage. She had promised her little brother a brighter future in school.

And if her fears turned out to be true, her family's situation would turn from bad to worse. Unfixable.

She placed her hand against her roiling stomach and swallowed.

How could Bernard have abandoned her in her time of need?

He had been so happy when she'd come to London that he dropped to his knees and proposed!

And now...

Now he refused to even speak to her. He let her sit on the wet doorstep, cold and alone, begging for an audience with him.

That was not the same man she'd fallen in love with.

The sweet melodies of your promises now ring hollow...

He might as well have been talking about himself in the letter.

"What am I going to do?" Emily whispered.

Astrid stilled, her lips pursed, her eyes narrowed before pulling out a piece of paper—no, a gossip column—from her pocket and nudging it toward Emily. "Perhaps *he* can help."

"What is that?" Emily wiped her wet hair away from her face before reluctantly taking the piece of paper into her hands.

The door opened then and the butler stepped out of the house. "Miss Astrid, your father is requesting your presence in his study. Immediately."

Emily resisted rolling her eyes. Cowards, the lot of them. Just a few minutes ago, this same butler had told her nobody was home.

"This is the column that ruined you." Astrid stood gingerly and shook out her skirts. "But perhaps it can offer salvation as well."

The swish of skirts, the receding footsteps, and then the decisive slam of the door told Emily that Astrid had left while she stared at the paper with an unseeing gaze.

This is the column that ruined you.

Emily was not certain she was ready to read the ugly words.

But perhaps it can offer salvation as well.

She had to be brave. If the column offered a solution Emily had not thought of, it was worth taking a look. She took a deep breath and read the words.

Dearest Reader,

Hold onto your bonnets and cravats, for this month's rake has recently returned to London and has already found himself embroiled in scandal.

Just yesterday morning, the infamous Mad Marquess—now ascended to the rank of a duke!—and his unruly friends unleashed a steam-powered carriage amongst the bustling streets of our beloved city. As constables attempted to halt this mechanical wonder the Mad Duke, as he is now titled, seized a pot of vibrant red paint from the ongoing town repairs and proceeded to paint the town red!

If that wasn't enough to stir the sensibilities of our genteel society, reports suggest that the daring Mad Duke publicly displayed his affections for an enchanting young lady, whispered to be Miss E—F —, the unmarried daughter of the late Baronet F—. In a blatant disregard for propriety, they engaged in a scandalous act right in the heart of the town square!

As audacious as it seems, it's neither the first nor, this author is quite certain, the last of the Mad Duke's escapades. After all, he didn't earn his nickname by following the rules.

The Mad Duke is infamous for his impetuous behavior, persistent indulgence in drinking, gambling, and promiscuity. He adamantly rejects the bonds of marriage, determined to drive his title into the ground. Any woman attempting to ensnare him is certain to be met with solitude and ruin.

This, however, doesn't dissuade the ladies from trying. Apart from possessing a coveted title, the Mad Duke boasts a strikingly handsome countenance, exhibits unparalleled skill in the saddle— both behind closed doors and on the race track—and let us not overlook his substantial fortune, rendering him irresistible for any woman.

Now, the pressing question remains: will the notorious Mad Duke extend the offer of his hand in marriage to rescue poor Miss E —F— from societal ruin, or will she join the ranks of the women he's abandoned?

Until next time, when the scandalous affairs of our brazen city unfold once more,

Yours unapologetically,
The Brazen Belle

Chapter Four

Bang. *Bang. Bang.*

Tyrone cracked open his burning eyelids. He shivered and his body sank lower into the lukewarm water. His face followed, water filling up his nostrils. *What the devil?*

Tyrone dove out, spitting out the liquid and sputtering, then took a lungful of air.

He looked around the marble room, his fingers digging into the copper bathtub, and blinked.

His throat was dry, his head was pounding, and his body felt as though he had been trampled by a herd of horses.

He lowered his hand over the rim of the bath, and his fingers touched the cool surface of a glass bottle.

Ah, the sweet feeling of salvation.

He picked up the bottle, pressed it to his lips, and tipped it up, marveling as the revitalizing liquid passed his lips, washed his mouth of the bitterness inside, and burned his throat. He felt like a thirsty man who had wandered the desert for thirty days and finally encountered an oasis.

Bang. Bang. Bang.

What the devil was that sound?

"Apologies, my lord." Bergen peeked his head inside the room. "I didn't think you were still—"

"What do you want?" Tyrone barked.

The valet gingerly stepped inside. "You have a guest, my lord."

"I am not home." Tyrone propped the back of his head against the cool bath surface and closed his eyes.

"It is a young lady, my lord," Bergen clarified.

Tyrone opened one eye. "Ah, that changes things." He felt drained, but perhaps a good roll in the sack would revitalize him. "Let her in."

The valet wrung his hands. "In here, my lord?"

Tyrone frowned. It wasn't the first time he'd invited a bawd into the house. Why was Bergen suddenly uncomfortable with the concept? "Yes, here."

The valet opened his mouth and then closed it again. His face grew a slightly darker shade of pink. "I do believe that the lady is... respectable."

Tyrone snorted. "Respectable? She might be playing respectable." But he paused to think. He didn't remember ordering a harlot. Then again, he didn't remember a lot of things. This woman could be dressed as a lady not to draw an eye to herself. Or perhaps it was a 'respectable' matron looking for a less than respectable way to spend an afternoon. Either way, now that he thought about it, he didn't fancy spending his time with the woman in the dirty, lukewarm tub of water. He needed to freshen up. "Very well. Tell her to wait in the drawing room. And bring me some clothes."

Tyrone didn't bother dressing up properly—he rarely did. If the woman waiting for him downstairs was a bawd, then he'd be undressed soon enough anyway. If she wasn't, then she'd be gone just as quickly. His waistcoat hung unbuttoned over his shirt, and his wet hair dripped onto his shoulders making the fabric cling to his body.

He slowly walked down the corridor and entered the drawing room.

A woman stood by the window, her back turned to him, looking out. She turned to face him the moment Tyrone entered the room.

She was a tiny little thing—not much in the way of a bosom —wrapped in a dull green gown and a dirty blue Spencer jacket. The skirt of the gown, which normally clung to a lady's rounded hips hung shapelessly from her waist. If she were indeed a harlot, she would not be one he would have chosen for himself. But as long as she was here...

"Good day," he said and walked toward the side table. He poured himself two fingers of whisky and took a sip before turning toward his guest.

"I apologize for interrupting your day," she said timidly. Her voice was pleasant and smooth, like the smoky whisky he'd just partaken in. He wondered how she might sound screaming from ecstasy.

"You did not," he said as his gaze slid down her gown again, imagining that perhaps the atrocious gown was hiding unknown pleasures. "Or at the very least, I don't mind this kind of inter-ruption."

A look of confusion passed her pale features. She was not the kind of woman he found attractive. Her lips were pressed into a thin line, her brows knitted in a frown, and her hair was hidden under a hideous-looking bonnet with a few short curls framing her rounded face. She looked like a prim governess. And while some men enjoyed playing the conquerors of virtuous women, Tyrone preferred his women loose. Unburdened. Passionate.

He would never turn her away, however. She was a woman. And there was no such thing as an unattractive woman to him. Plain looking, certainly. But some primal instinct within him still wanted to unwrap her and see what was beyond those clothes.

He swallowed, his voice thick with rising passion. "Come here and spread your lovely thighs."

The look of confusion and horror that flashed in her eyes was almost tangible. "Pardon me?" He could've sworn she sounded offended.

"Oh, I shall pardon you if that's what you want. Or I can punish you." He waggled his eyebrows suggestively as he propped his hips against the side table and patted his knee. "Come here."

"I beg your pardon!" The woman's pale face turned dark red. Her lips trembled, and she seemed incapable of intelligible thought for one long moment. Then her features turned thunderous. "I am not here to suffer your rude behavior."

Tyrone's worst fear had materialized. This woman was not here to pleasure him.

He took another sip of his drink.

But that made no sense! Why else would a woman cross the threshold of his house? "Then why are you here?"

She squinted at him, her lips pursed in indignation. "You do not remember me at all, do you? Why should you? You were well into your cups when we met last—"

"Apologies, love," he cut her off as his nagging headache only worsened from the inflow of her words. "But I am not much into remembering faces. Now if we talk about what's under those skirts—"

She seemed to choke on air. "How dare you!"

He rolled his eyes and waved a dismissing hand. "Already bored." He pressed a cool glass to his aching forehead.

"I demand you apologize to me this instant!" she cried.

Tyrone wasn't looking at the woman anymore, but in his mind's eye, he could easily imagine her outraged expression. "I shall do no such thing."

"I did not come here to listen to your vulgarities!"

Tyrone downed the remainder of his whisky, placed the

empty glass on the side table, and regarded the seething lady. "If you did not come here to... well, come, then why are you here?"

She scrunched up her face as if trying to decipher his words but finally gave up. When she spoke, every word came out bitingly through her teeth. "My name is Miss Emily Fitzwilliam."

Tyrone watched her steadily. "I shan't remember that."

"And I came here to demand you marry me."

Now it was Tyrone's turn to choke on air. He wished he still had whisky in his hands, but somehow lacked the necessary strength to pour himself another glass. Instead, he crossed his arms over his chest and his feet at his ankles. Marry her! *Pft!* "Marry you? What madness has befallen you? I shall do no such thing under *any* circumstances."

"But you have to!" She looked so certain. As though *he* was the unreasonable one, not her.

"Why would I do that?" he asked through his teeth.

She straightened her shoulders. "Because you ruined me."

He leaned forward and squinted at her waist. Was that why she was wearing this shapeless gown? Had he impregnated this lady and didn't even remember it?

He did have numerous lovers, but he was always careful. He always used the armor. *Always.*

Then again, he didn't even remember her.

He glanced at her face once more.

She did look familiar. But now that he studied her closely, now that he'd spoken to her, he recognized her bearing to be undeniably genteel.

She was a gentleman's daughter. And Tyrone did not frolic with gentle ladies. Not unmarried ones, anyway.

How had this happened? "Ruined you?" His throat was dry, and his voice came out rather hoarse.

"Yes!" She rummaged through her pocket, then took out a piece of paper—a gossip column?—and nudged it toward him.

Tyrone took a step and cautiously grabbed the newspaper

cutout from her. He scanned the words, and finally, everything became clear.

That's where he remembered her from!

He'd tackled her away from the steam carriage's path. His confidence returning, he met her gaze. "I saved you."

"And in the process of saving me, you ruined me," she countered.

He narrowed his eyes at her. "Would you rather be dead?"

"I'd rather be married," she answered without missing a beat.

Tyrone almost laughed. He had to hand it to the young miss. She had gumption and resolve. Under any other circumstances, they could have been friends.

"And I'd rather not." He walked toward the hearth and threw the crumpled paper into the fire. "Marrying a duke. What a lovely opportunity, isn't it?"

"You think I *want* to marry you?" She sounded repulsed by the notion. "You think I am looking forward to the prospect?"

"You are here, aren't you?" He raised a brow and leaned one shoulder against the hearth.

"I am only here as a last resort." She waved a hand toward the flames. "The paper you so cavalierly burnt has destroyed my life, my family. I had a loving fiancé, you see, who now refuses to even speak to me because of that hurtful article. My sisters are doomed to wear the mantle of ruined women because of something that happened to *me*! And my brother—"

"If your fiancé was indeed *loving*," Tyrone mocked the mere notion with his tone as he interrupted the long tirade, "then why won't he marry you now? He can save your reputation, you know."

Her face turned crimson, her hands fisted at her sides as her entire body stiffened. If he didn't know better, he'd have thought she was going to explode. "Because men are despicable!"

He let out a snort. "Well, I certainly am not going to disprove that."

She opened her mouth and stood there frozen for a long moment. So long, in fact, that Tyrone was beginning to think she had frozen in place. "How can you call yourself a gentleman when you refuse to help a lady in trouble?" she finally asked, her voice pleasantly hoarse.

Sun filtered through the window, bathing the room in a glow of color.

He smiled lazily and shook his head. He was enjoying himself, he realized. "I never said I was a gentleman."

"Please," she breathed. He could see that she was not a lady used to begging. But begging she was. "I shall do anything you want."

"Anything?" He cocked a brow as he studied her form suggestively, his tongue tracing his upper lip.

"Anything." Her words were firm.

He narrowed his eyes, and a sly smile touched his lips. "Then I want you to leave and never return."

Chapter Five

Emily exited the house and took a moment to collect her wits. She inhaled deeply and bit her lip to keep it from trembling. She'd failed again.

The carriage door opened, and the Earl of Sutton jumped out, approaching her swiftly and offering his arm. "It didn't go well, I take it."

Emily shook her head and gripped his forearm, slowly making her way down the stairs and into his waiting carriage. "It did not. He refuses to have any association with me."

The earl nodded and gently handed her into the carriage, then settled across from her.

She looked out the window, wondering if more scandal was going to follow her after it became known that she was gallivanting around town in the earl's carriage, and without a chaperone. Could one be more ruined than she already was? She had no money, no prospects, only scandal.

"Do not worry, Miss Fitzwilliam," the earl said as if sensing her turmoil. "You shall have a bridegroom by the end of this week."

Emily was not convinced, but she was grateful for the attempt. "Thank you for helping me."

"No need to thank me," he answered with a smile as he rapped the roof of the carriage, prompting it to a start.

"Oh, yes, there is. I cannot fathom why you would do this for me when you have absolutely no incentive to do so." She turned toward him and something in his expression made her add, "Unless, you do."

The earl laughed hoarsely. "You are quite perceptive. And very clever. Not to mention agreeable, polite, and charming. And those are the reasons why I am helping you."

"Because I am charming?" Emily raised her brow.

He chuckled again. "I made a few inquiries about you after the incident, and some more after that paper came out and plunged you into ruin. And I think you shall be a good fit as a wife to my friend."

"You do?" Emily remembered the disheveled, drunken duke and wondered how she would be a good fit for him. "What have you learned that led you to this conclusion, may I ask?"

"Certainly. I learned that your father was a baronet, which means you are a part of the gentry and capable of running estates. I learned that you have three younger siblings and an ailing mother whom you've been looking after since your father's death. I know that you basically took over your father's land that your brother will inherit in ten-odd years because your guardian is rather useless. You're a very determined young lady, firmly planted on your feet. And I think your influence would be beneficial to my friend. He has the power to save you from ruination, but perhaps you have the means to save him from his demons."

An involuntary laugh left her lips. "I am not looking to save anyone, my lord. Except for my family, of course, and myself."

He nodded thoughtfully. "Your family is very important to you, isn't it?"

"They are everything," she said emphatically.

41

"Well, your husband will be your family, too." He shrugged. "At least, I hope you shall come to see it that way."

"I am sorry, my lord. I do not mean to give you false hope. But I don't believe in miracle rescues. And I don't believe that a woman can save a man from his own vices. Especially if he is not willing to save himself. I cannot promise you that I shall expend my energy on that endeavor." Perhaps she should have lied and told the earl that she would do her best, that she would try to save his friend so that he'd try even harder to push the duke to marry her. Except she couldn't lie to the man who was trying to help her. She couldn't lie, period. It was one of her major flaws.

"Be that as it may," the earl said over the loud rattle of the carriage. "Some men need but a nudge. I hope you shall come to appreciate my friend Tyrone for more than his shortcomings. You're more than your ruined reputation, Miss Fitzwilliam. And he is more than his scandalous one."

Emily chewed her lower lip in thought before raising her face to the earl's. "Couldn't... *you* marry me instead?"

She'd been gathering the courage to ask him that from the moment she appeared on his doorstep. And she fully expected him to laugh in her face.

Instead, his face took on a pained expression. "I would have done it in a heartbeat," he said, his eyes glinting with some unfathomable feeling. "Alas, I am already married."

Tyrone had been waiting for Steeplechase races for as long as he could remember.

Horse riding had been his escape ever since he was a child. He loved racing. He was good at it, and he was praised for it. In fact, it was the only thing his father had ever approved of when it concerned him.

Not only was riding his favorite pastime, but as Steeplechase races were an Irish invention, they brought on pleasant memories of his homeland. And he didn't have a lot of those.

Most reminders that place brought were rotten. And rot was exactly what he was willing to let the lands do in his absence. He wasn't ever going back home. That just was not going to happen.

But he wasn't going to miss these races. He—and by he, he meant his money—helped organize this event, after all. He even brought his prized mare, and he was going to race it himself.

He uncorked his flask and took a swig of whisky, then wiped his mouth with his sleeve.

"Are you certain you want to drink before the race?" came a familiar female voice.

Tyrone turned slowly and beheld Miss Emma... something. He didn't remember her last name. He wasn't certain he correctly remembered her first name either. The only thing he remembered was that she was an extremely desperate miss who'd begged him to marry her.

"I shall drink after, so what difference does it make?" He looked around, trying to figure out what this woman was doing here. How did she even get here? He'd thought he was rid of her.

"I think the difference is between finishing on top of the horse or being dragged across the finish line," she said rather matter-of-factly.

Tyrone snorted. "What would you know about any of that?"

"I won't pretend to know much about racing," she said bitingly. "But I would imagine that falling off a horse would hurt more than being tumbled against the cobblestones by a duke."

"I doubt you know anything about being tumbled," he grumbled under his breath. "What are you doing here, Miss Desperate?"

"Miss Fitzwilliam," she corrected evenly, seemingly unperturbed that she was creating even more scandal by appearing at the races and approaching him here. "And to ask one more time if perhaps you'd reconsider your stance against marrying me."

"Never," he vowed and took another swig of whisky. "And I remember you telling me you'd do anything and then not keeping your promise to never bother me again."

"I said I'd do anything if you agreed to marry me. So, I will gladly leave you alone and never bother you again but only *after* you marry me."

He raised his eyes heavenward. "Miss F... Fortune. Ah, yes, I think this name suits you best. *Misfortune.* And you shall have to find another victim. Because I am not moved by your plight."

She curled her hands into fists. "What if we came to an arrangement, Your... Disgrace?"

He let out a chuckle. At least, she was entertaining. "What kind of arrangement?"

"Well..." She frowned. "If we marry, I shall not disturb your lifestyle and shall allow you to continue your debauched ways."

He let out a snort. "I can continue my debauched ways without you."

"I can..." She pursed her lips adorably in thought. "I will be a perfect mistress for your estates."

"My estates do not need a mistress. They take care of themselves." He flicked an invisible piece of lint off his jacket. "What else can you offer?"

"I shall..." She narrowed her eyes, and her cheeks flooded with color. "You need heirs, don't you? I shall provide you with as many children as you'd like."

He raised a brow. He wasn't interested in extending the Tyrone line. He would be happy if his legacy as a duke died with him. But he was curious how far she was willing to go. So he stepped closer, pressing his advantage. "You will allow me to bed you whenever I like?"

She swallowed. "Whenever you like."

"Be it day or night, in bed or out of it, inside the house or outside?"

She faltered. "O-outside?"

He nodded. "Mhhmm." He towered over her.

She lowered her eyes. "W-why would anyone want to do it outside? And h-how does—"

Tyrone chucked her under her chin, forcing her to meet his gaze. "Answer. The. Question."

She swallowed hard. "I-I shall perform my wifely duties to the best of my ability."

He smirked, taking a couple of steps back. "Have you no pride?"

"Pride?" Her timidity disappearing, anger took its place. "I cannot afford pride! I would sell it if I could, only there are no takers. But you wouldn't understand. You were born a duke—"

"I was born a marquess, actually," he interrupted cavalierly.

"More importantly, you were born a man!" Her face was red now, and her eyes glinted with frustration as she paced in a tiny circle, limping slightly. "How are you to know what it's like to be a female, looking out for everyone when the estate your little brother inherited barely pays for itself? And I have to run the household with a single maid, a brood of siblings, and an ailing mother. How can you talk about pride when—" She paused, then her eyes rounded in horror.

Tyrone blinked and looked around in search of whom he owed his thanks to for making the woman stop her tirade. Then he followed her gaze as she looked down and pursed his lips, trying very hard not to laugh at the woman's misfortune.

She calmly took a step back and shook out her foot. "—when all I do is step on horse crap, apparently."

Tyrone couldn't hold his laughter any longer, he let out a bark, his hand on his chest. "But you manage to do it with dignity. Well, it was entertaining talking to you, if nothing else." He waved his hat and approached his horse, ready to be rid of the woman. She was tenacious, obstinate, and absolutely tantalizing.

Tantalizing? Where did that come from? Sure, there was

45

something about her big, brown, doe eyes that called to him. She didn't cower in fear from him and she cared for her family...

Or perhaps she used her family as leverage to secure herself a titled husband.

Yes, Tyrone was certain that was it. And as intriguing as sparring with her had been, he had more important things to take care of.

Sutton appeared by her side at that moment and finally, things started making sense.

"Ah, Judas," Tyrone said and took a swig of his whisky. "You're the one who brought her here."

"Yes," Sutton answered unperturbed. "But I am doing it for your own good."

"Of course." Tyrone nodded. Sutton had been trying to keep him on the straight and narrow ever since he returned home.

"And I can't stand idly by when a lady needs my assistance," the traitor continued. "Tyrone, have a heart. She has no prospects because of our carelessness."

"If you're this worried about her, why don't you marry her?" Tyrone winked and got on his horse. "Then you can lock her up at one of your estates and continue your carefree life. Oh... wait a moment. Didn't you already do that?"

Sutton took a menacing step. "Don't you dare—"

Tyrone waved a dismissive hand. "Oh, I would never stick my nose in your business; that's your territory. Miss Fortune." He tipped his hat. "It was a pleasure... Actually, it wasn't. I hope we shall never meet again. Good day."

"Mad Duke! Mad Duke! Mad Duke!" The air around him was filled with tension as every person in the stands chanted for his successful completion of the race.

He was not going to win, but despite some people's predictions, he was going to finish the race unscathed. The exhilaration of the race, the wind in his face, and the sounds of cheering always made him feel alive.

Tyrone crossed the finish line and stretched out his arms in victory.

He stopped the horse and tried to concentrate on the crowd of onlookers, searching for Miss... whatever her name was. She wasn't there and neither was Sutton.

So, they'd left. Good. That's all he wanted.

"Mad Duke! Mad Duke! Mad Duke!"

His gaze stopped as he saw a gorgeous woman on the edge of the crowd. She was wearing a deep violet gown and her eyes, as green as his, were fixed on him. Her hair was collected atop her head, no hat in sight. And her features were so familiar... Just as he remembered her.

The sounds receded to the background and all went quiet for a long moment.

Was it a dream? Tyrone tried to walk toward her, completely forgetting that he was still atop a horse.

The world moved, and everything whirled around him. The next thing he knew, Tyrone was lying on the ground, as a few people ran toward him.

Tyrone frantically searched the stands for the woman he'd just seen, but his vision was blurry.

Had he truly seen her?

Was she truly there?

He feared he would never find out, for in the next moment, everything went black.

Chapter Six

Tyrone sat up sharply, water dripping down his face.

Why was water dripping down his face? He blinked and scrubbed his face with his hands. A man crouched before him with a flask.

"Are you well?"

Am I?

He looked around, searching for the woman in his vision, his pulse pounding at his temples.

It felt like a dream. It had to be. She wasn't real. She couldn't be.

Tyrone got up on shaky legs and scrubbed his face once more, his beard poking at his palms. He needed a shave. How long had it been since he'd shaved?

He didn't remember. He'd never cared about shaving before. Now, everything aggravated him.

He turned around and... froze.

Before him stood his vision.

The woman he'd noticed in the stands before.

She stood tall and straight like a lance. Like she always did.

Her green eyes glinted with unshed tears, giving her face a look of perpetual sadness. Like they always did.

So fucking familiar, it hurt.

"Xander," she said in her low and gentle voice. Just as he remembered it. And that lovely sound was like a punch in the gut.

She slowly approached him, and as she did, he could see her more clearly. She had barely changed. Sure, there was gray in her hair, her face lacked the roundness of youth, and laugh lines were prominent in the corners of her eyes and around her mouth. Laugh lines.

He had barely seen her laugh. He didn't even remember the sound.

"What the devil are you doing here?" he barked.

Those familiar eyes fell closed for a moment, and she inhaled deeply. "I came to see you."

"Then you wasted your time." His throat was so dry he had to clear it.

She wrung her hands. "I thought we could start anew."

He let out a bitter laugh, his head giving a sharp ache. He ignored it. The ache in his heart overshadowed any other ailments. "Are you in half-mourning?" He tipped his head toward her gown. "Playing a grieving widow, are we?"

"A grieving mother," she corrected softly.

Tyrone scoffed. "A mother? Is that what you call yourself? You haven't been a mother for decades. Not since you left us... Left *me*. Alone with him."

"You were his heir." She took a step forward, her hand outstretched.

A few years ago, he would have given anything to take her hand, to rub his face against her soft palm. If only she'd come a few years earlier.

"I couldn't take you with me," she continued. "He would have come for us. He would have killed me."

Tyrone nodded. "Right. So you left me behind to gain your freedom. Well, the freedom is yours."

"I couldn't come earlier. You know that!" she cried. "But I came for you now. The moment I heard of his death—"

"I don't need you here," he snapped. "I needed you when he was alive. When he was beating me half to death if I did anything wrong. Or even if I did something right. If I reminded him of *you*." His voice broke on the last word, and she reared back as if he'd slapped her. "I don't need you now. You're nothing to me."

"I am still a duchess," she said in a shaking whisper. "Even if you don't need me, the dukedom does. It needs a mistress."

There was a long pause as he watched his mother standing before him like an apparition. But she was real. Flesh and blood.

And she had come here to assume her rightful place as the duchess.

When she'd left, his heart had grown cold until it turned to ice. Now, he thought he felt it thaw. Or perhaps it was just a reminder that it could still hurt. *He* could still be hurt.

He turned away and mumbled under his breath, "Not for long."

~

"This is the last of it," Harriet said as she brought a small trunk downstairs. "Sophie is helping Reggie gather his things, but our chamber is all gathered up and ready."

"Good." Emily nodded and looked around the tiny cottage. She wouldn't miss it, but she was loath to leave so soon.

When they were getting ready to leave for London, she had promised her sisters the world, a brighter future. And now, they were running away with their tails tucked between their legs.

She'd received a letter this morning from Sutton. Failing to secure her a husband, he was willing to take her in as a companion for his wife. It was not a perfect arrangement, but a lot better than nothing.

Emily worried that Harriet would not be able to assume all of Emily's responsibilities. All the siblings would have to grow up fast. And in a few years, Harriet would need to seek a position, too. Because marriage prospects were now closed to them all.

But at least, they wouldn't starve. And Emily would be hidden away from scandal—the current scandal and the one that was about to come.

"Do you want me to—?" Harriet started but was interrupted by a sharp knock on the door.

Emily and Harriet exchanged a curious glance. Who could it be? Another missive from Lord Sutton, perhaps?

Another rap. More forceful this time.

Her heart drumming in her chest, Emily hurried toward the door.

The rapping intensified.

Who was this impatient person? She threw the door open and gasped.

Whoever she imagined she would see behind the door, well, she was wrong.

There stood a tall—very tall, Emily had to crane her neck to look at him—and rather handsome young gentleman. He paused, his arm raised as if ready to strike the door again.

He was impeccably dressed in all black save for the crisp white shirt and cravat, his coat snuggly hugging his powerful, broad shoulders.

He had a straight aristocratic nose, sharp cheekbones, and a chiseled jawline. And his wavy jet-black hair curled at the bottom, softly caressing his shoulders.

There was something familiar about him, but also something very foreign and even exotic. He was like a prince from the fairy tales, the ones she used to read as a child with illustrations. And for a moment, Emily fancied herself the heroine of one of those tales, falling madly in love at first sight.

The *Prince's* emerald green eyes glinted with some unfathomable emotion, and his full lips thinned into a single line.

He straightened and tugged on the lapels of his ironed-out coat. "Do you not have a butler?"

His voice immediately brought Emily out of her daze and into reality. He was not a prince from a fairy tale. Far from it. This was the Duke of Tyrone!

Emily took a step back from the shock of the realization.

He looked extremely different from the two times she'd seen him. His beard was gone, his hair was combed and styled in a way that didn't make him look like a sixty-year-old vagabond who hadn't cleaned himself in weeks. He looked... respectable. And young! She'd known he was young, but now he looked like it.

"Are you going to let me in or should I stand here all day?" he barked, and the remnants of shock faded away along with the dreams of love at first sight.

Her fingers curled into fists and she craved to throw him out on his arse, the way he had done when she came to his house.

But he was a duke. And if he'd lowered his pompous self to come to her little cottage, perhaps he had something important to say.

"Please, come in," she said as politely as she could muster and opened the door wider.

He stepped inside and looked around, contempt evident on his face.

"Not the palatial grandeur you are used to," Emily said scathingly and closed the door behind him. "Please, proceed into our drawing room."

She curtsied mockingly all the while smiling sweetly at him.

He didn't look amused. "After you."

"Of course." Emily walked toward the only room that was acceptable enough to entertain a guest.

"Harriet, be a dear and bring the duke some tea, please," Emily said as they passed the stairs where her sister still stood, frozen, her mouth gaping open.

Harriet didn't move a muscle.

The duke threw a glance toward her before turning to Emily. "Your butler doesn't open the door, and your maid is not listening to your commands. What kind of household do you run?"

Emily straightened her spine. "One without a butler and a maid. This is my sister. Harriet. Harriet, this is the Duke of Tyrone."

Harriet seemed to awaken from her stupor and dropped into a curtsy. "A pleasure, my lord—pardon, Your Grace."

"Please, bring us some tea," Emily repeated with a gentle smile when the duke ignored Harriet's polite greeting.

Instead, he entered their drawing room and started stalking around the tiny room like a caged panther. With his gaze, he studied every little crack in the walls and glowered at every creak of the floorboards. "This is where you live," he said, rather than asked, when Emily stepped into the room.

He dwarfed the tiny room even more, and there was barely any room for Emily to breathe. And his energetic strides felt out of place in the comfort of this quiet place.

"We are renting this cottage for the duration of our stay in London," Emily answered with her head raised proudly. "But we are leaving. Today."

He threw her a menacing frown. "You're leaving."

"Indeed." Emily straightened her shoulders.

He continued pacing in silence, his hands locked behind his back.

"This is what you wanted, wasn't it? Me gone. Away from you and your unwed self?"

He still didn't say anything.

Emily let out a frustrated breath. "Would you mind telling me why you are here?"

He turned on her sharply. "Is your father home?"

Emily narrowed her eyes on him. *My father?* "He's been dead for three years now." Perhaps not the most polite way to impart the information, but she was getting exceedingly annoyed with the duke.

"What about a brother? A guardian?" His voice took on a squeaking quality on the last word, and he had to clear his throat and tug on his cravat.

"My brother, Reggie, is eleven years old. Would you like to speak to him?" she asked sweetly and fluttered her eyelashes for good measure.

He absently waved a careless hand and resumed his pacing. "Then I shall speak to you."

"How lovely." Her voice was void of emotion.

"I've spent a lot of time since we last saw each other thinking about the predicament that you're in."

"That was yesterday," she pointed out. "And since you were greatly in your cups, I doubt you were conscious enough to think for more than an hour since our last encounter."

"Do you have to interrupt?" he snapped irritably. "I am trying to tell you something."

Emily let out a scoff and waved a hand for him to proceed.

"I spent a great deal of time thinking," he repeated emphatically. "And I decided that I shall marry you."

There was a loud clatter behind them, and Emily turned to see that Harriet had overturned the tea tray. "Oh!" She dropped to her knees trying to clean it up, but her eyes darted from the duke to Emily.

Emily rushed toward her to make certain she didn't burn or cut herself on the ruined tea set.

"A duchess?" Harriet whispered, her eyes feverish. "You are going to be a duchess!"

Emily helped Harriet collect all the broken pieces back onto the tray and shooed her away. Her mind was reeling and dashing from one thought to the next.

She stood and dusted her skirts, trying to collect her wits before turning back to the duke.

"You need to learn some etiquette if you're to become my wife," he said in bored tones. "My stables are run with more grace than this house."

Emily squinted at the duke. "Would you mind repeating that?"

He cocked a brow. "My stables are—"

"No, no." Emily let out a huff of laughter. "Not that. The part about you marrying me."

"Oh, that." He cleared his throat and tugged on his perfectly tied cravat. "Due to the situation that we've found ourselves in, I find it prudent that we marry."

She shook her head, trying to dispel all the thoughts that tumbled one after the other in her mind. "When I came to you, you said that would never happen. You humiliated me and cursed me."

A light twitch of his lips was, perhaps, an indication of his remorse or displeasure. She didn't know which. "I did not curse you. I simply didn't take into consideration all the variables."

"Yesterday, you said you never wanted to see me again."

He swallowed. "I was in my cups."

"And you're not now?" She raised a brow.

"Am I to understand you're refusing my offer?"

Emily crossed her arms over her chest. "I believe I haven't heard an offer as of yet."

The duke let out a little huff of laughter before mirroring her position. "Fine. Here it is. We shall marry. But you're not to interfere with my life."

She was to marry this drunkard and reprobate—the man who ruined her life and smeared her name—and not make any noise?

Emily felt her blood boil. She didn't usually get riled up easily, but lately, she couldn't contain her emotions. "I can't promise that."

"What do you mean you can't promise that?" The duke looked sincerely baffled.

"You want me to promise to sit idly by while you continue your debauchery and not say a word. Well, that is just not who I am. If I think you're making a mistake or doing something wrong, I shall have my say. I am the eldest sibling in my household, I can't just—"

He cut her off with a sharp gesture of his hand. "I don't care. I am saving you from ruination and—"

"Saving me?" Emily fisted her hands by her side so she wouldn't try to strangle the arrogant man. "You're the reason I am ruined!"

"Listen here, pet—"

"I am *not* your pet."

"I came here to offer you a deal. I don't have to marry you. You have no choice *but* to marry me."

She took a deep breath trying to calm herself. He was right, and she knew it. Without him, she was ruined. But she could not promise something she would not be able to deliver. If he continued his scandalous ways, it could hurt her sisters' chances of advantageous matches and they were one of the main reasons she even wanted to get married.

Besides, something had changed. Despite what he might have wanted her to believe, he wasn't here out of the goodness of his heart. She knew him enough to know that he needed this marriage for his own selfish reasons. The question was, how much? "I promise to not intervene in the aspects of your life that do not involve me."

He blinked. "As far as the concessions go, this isn't the best one."

She raised her chin, her teeth chattering lightly. "This is the best I can do."

He took a couple of steps forward, which in this tiny room brought them almost toe to toe. "I do not want you meddling in my affairs. After we marry, you will be conveyed to my estate in Ireland, and you are not to come to England unless I call upon you."

The gall! Emily shook her head. "I can't agree to that."

The duke raised his eyes heavenward. "I'm sorry, are you just used to disagreeing all the time?"

"I have two sisters who will soon need to be introduced into society, to marry," Emily insisted. She needed to make him understand. "And a little brother who needs to learn how to run his estate once he reaches his majority. They are the only reason I am even entertaining the idea of marrying you." There was a glimmer of something in the duke's eyes akin to curiosity and something else, something Emily did not dare identify. She plowed on, "If I were alone, I would rather be ruined than shackled to a person I do not love—do not know—or as is the case between us, a person I do not particularly like. But when you ruined me, you ruined the future of my siblings, too. And if I am to marry, I need to correct their standing in society. I need to make certain they can have advantageous marriages. I need to find my brother a tutor. And for that, I need to be a part of society. I shall need to sponsor them onto the marriage mart. I need to buy them new gowns, and slippers, and—"

"With my money, I presume?" His face hardened once more.

"With whatever allowance you allocate me." She swallowed. "I am not going to empty your coffers if that's your worry. But I need to be in London during the social season. And—"

"Fine." He cut her off with an abrupt gesture. "You can do whatever you want. I shall allocate you a generous allowance. Generous by your standards, anyway," he said as he looked around the room with a grimace of distaste. "And then you shall leave me the hell alone."

Emily opened her mouth to respond, and he impatiently

raised his hand. "By God, woman, you can't be disagreeing again! I agreed to give you everything you want."

Emily clamped her lips shut and glared at the duke. He was right. He'd given her everything she'd wanted. Which meant that *she* was right as well. He needed this marriage almost as much as she did.

Why?

She shook the question away. She wasn't about to look a gift horse in the mouth.

His grimace turned smug as he straightened, smoothing his cravat with his gloved hand. "Splendid. I shall get a special license and we'll be married by the end of the week." He flew past her, almost toppling over Harriet as she entered the room with a plate of biscuits in one hand and a rag in another. He threw her a brief nod and stormed out of the house.

Harriet blinked, looking from the now-empty doorway to a stunned Emily.

"I suppose we are staying in London," Emily said with a nervous chuckle. "And we need to get ready for the wedding."

Chapter Seven

"I take thee, Alexander Blackwood, the Duke of Tyrone, to be my wedded husband, to have and to hold from this day forward." His bride's solemn voice enveloped him like a soft and cozy blanket.

Tyrone held her gloves hands in his, running his thumb over her knuckles. Her hands were warm and something equally as warm unfurled inside his chest.

Voices buzzed around him, wrenching him out of his thoughts.

"Let's have another drink!" a slurred voice boomed, followed by loud cheering. Where was that coming from?

Tyrone blinked, and the sun hit his eyes, forcing him to squint once again. He needed to concentrate. He had just been holding his bride's hands...

"For better for worse, for richer for poorer, in sickness and in health..." There it was, her voice, again. It soothed his aching soul.

He looked into her deep brown eyes and saw sadness in them.

She had pursued him so relentlessly. He'd thought today would be the happiest day of her life. The day she snagged a duke. He'd expected to see a happy smile on her face, or at the very least, a fiendish smirk. But no.

She was pale, the color drained from her cheeks. Her lips were blue and trembling. And her face was... blank. The face of resignation.

"To the groom!" someone shouted, distracting Tyrone's attention. The male voices were distorted in the background, and the lights flickered all around them while he and his new bride were plunged into darkness.

Yet her voice continued, solemn and void of emotion, "To love, cherish, and obey, so long as we both shall live."

Loud music started playing around them, as people danced, laughing and cheering. Then the atmosphere changed in an instant.

The sounds of fists connecting with flesh grabbed his attention. Was someone fighting?

Tyrone picked up a tankard and slammed it against someone's head. He swayed on his feet and the next thing he knew, he was staring at the ceiling.

What was happening?

It all grew eerily quiet all of a sudden. But the darkness fell away and instead, a sharp light penetrated his eyelids. He squinted and turned away, throwing his arm over his eyes.

Ah, there she was again. His sad but beautiful bride.

She was staring at him with that empty gaze of hers. But after a few moments of silence, she raised her brows, as if questioning him or expecting something.

He looked to the right, at the minister, and he had the same questioning look in his eyes.

"Your turn, Your Grace," he said with a nod. "Repeat after me."

Tyrone nodded.

"With this ring, I thee wed," the minister said.

Tyrone looked down at his hands. He didn't have a ring. He didn't even think he needed a ring for this. Could they not get married without rings?

"With my body, I thee worship," the minister continued.

Tyrone squeezed his fingers around his bride's hands. He could not give his body to her. At least, not fully. Was he allowed to lie in the vows? Why was he suddenly bothered by it?

"And with all my worldly goods, I thee endow."

This part, he could say. He didn't mind sharing his wealth, after all.

Tyrone opened his mouth to repeat the words but nothing came out. His mouth was dry and no matter how hard he tried, no sound emerged.

With all my worldly goods, I thee endow!

Tyrone screamed the words in his mind, but his lips refused to cooperate, his throat refused to let out the sounds.

"Aargh!" Tyrone let out a scream only to sit up in bed.

He blinked a few times, his breathing labored, trying to get used to the brightly illuminated room.

He should learn to close the drapes before going to bed.

He averted his eyes from the windows and threw the sheet off.

He paused at an unexpected discovery.

He was still clothed, his shirt was buttoned, and he even had a waistcoat on. But that wasn't the surprising part. What caught him off guard was the fact that his breeches rode down on his hips and the falls of the breeches were undone.

What had happened last night? He didn't remember much.

He remembered getting married... Or was it a dream? He couldn't quite make out which part was reality and which was not. It wasn't the first time that had happened, either.

Perhaps he should give up the drink.

Tyrone smirked. As if that was ever going to happen. At least, not while he was still in England, on his father's properties.

He scrambled from the bed and stretched, his eyes catching more and more of the room.

Wait a moment, I'm not even in my bedchamber!

It was the duchess's chamber!

Now things slowly started making sense. He had spent the

night in his wife's room... and his falls were undone. This meant that—

The door handle rattled and the door opened, revealing his wife as she walked into the room. She took a couple of steps before pausing. Her eyes wide, she looked as bewildered as Tyrone felt. Then her gaze dropped down his body, and her mouth fell open.

Tyrone followed her gaze, and his cheeks burnt in embarrassment.

Fuck. His breeches hung around his hips, and his crotch was completely naked to her view. He quickly jumped to pull up his breeches and buttoned up.

"Apologies!" His wife turned away as if that would help her unsee what she'd already witnessed. "I... uh... I didn't mean to stare."

"No need to apologize," he answered. "It's not like you haven't seen it before."

"Yes, I certainly have. If you'll excuse me." She hurried away and locked herself in her dressing room.

Had she gone there to hide from him? Well, if she'd thought that he'd leave her alone, she was mistaken. They needed to talk. Tyrone needed to make certain he hadn't made the greatest mistake of his life last night. If he bedded her, he, at the very least, should have used precautions. But he couldn't see the evidence of that anywhere in the room.

His wife returned a few moments later, looking rather pale. Her eyes were sunken, and her cheeks lacked any color. She'd washed her face, he realized by the wet strands of golden-brown hair curling by her temples. The rest of her hair was pinned rather strangely to her head, not that he was a master of coiffures. She looked at him as if she'd expected him to be gone by now.

"Are you unwell?" he asked.

"Hm?" She raised her eyebrow in question.

"You look..." Was it rude to point out her pallor? He decided to change tactics. "Had a little too much to drink last night, did you?"

"No." She shook her head and crossed her arms over her chest. "I believe that was you."

He let out a snort. "I certainly shall not deny that."

She wrung her hands. "Since you're here, I was hoping we could discuss the matter of my allowance. You said that—"

"In a moment." Tyrone stopped her with a gesture of his hand. "First, I would love to discuss what happened last night."

She blinked in confusion. "Last night?"

"Yes, we slept together and—"

She scoffed. "Oh, no, we haven't slept together. Or at least, I haven't slept a wink!"

A little smile tugged at his lips. "I kept you up all night, huh?"

"Oh, yes." She nodded. "And if we're to discuss this, then perhaps I could ask you not to come to my bed when you're in your cups."

She looked rather angry. Had he not taken the time to pleasure her? He could be rather selfish when under the influence of liquor, and to be honest, he was surprised he'd kept her awake all night. He must have enjoyed her company.

"Apologies if I was a little rough."

"A *little* rough?" A frown gathered between her brows. "Not only did you wake me up in the middle of the night when you came to my bedroom, but you refused to let me sleep afterward. The moment I slipped into slumber, you would pull me out."

But did I pull myself out? He couldn't quite ask the important question. But if they indeed engaged in intercourse more than once there was an even bigger chance that he had been far less careful than he should have been.

He scratched his jaw. "Did I take any precautions?"

She squinted in confusion. "Precautions?"

"Did I... wear anything?"

She looked around the room. "Your coat is on the armchair over there."

Tyrone pursed his lips. He would have to be more direct than that. "I mean the armor."

"The armor? Why would you—" She looked him up and down slowly. "You are large as it is! I am all sore now; my entire body aches because of you! If you wore the armor—"

Tyrone raised his arm to halt her, caught between laughter and remorse. He *was* quite large. Women had told him that often enough for him to know it was the truth. The armor would not add much to his girth, however. But she had likely been a virgin up until last night and probably didn't know that. And if she ached that badly this morning, it meant he had brutishly taken her virtue, failing to prepare her properly.

Of course, she'd think that armor would hurt even more. "I am sorry. I don't exactly remember what happened. I was rather drunk. I assure you, next time it won't be as painful. But I need to know—"

"Next time?" She took a step back and raised her hands as if in self-defense. "No, no, there won't be a next time. I know that married couples spend their nights together, but I would prefer it if you used your own chamber."

Tyrone frowned in confusion. "What?"

"What?" she echoed.

Tyrone let out a sigh. "Never mind that. I apologize for being rough. And I shouldn't have bothered you through the entire night, but I was drunk."

"That is exactly the problem, isn't it?" She pressed her fists to her sides.

"I am usually more attentive than this, even when drunk, I promise. But... You didn't enjoy it even a little?" He shouldn't have been concentrating on that part. But he had to admit, his ego was bruised.

"Enjoy it? That's what I am trying to tell you. It was terrible!"

"Terrible?"

"The sounds you made were... animalistic."

"I made sounds?"

"Yes! Terrible, awful sounds. And the smell!"

Tyrone swallowed, his cheeks burning from humiliation. "Now listen here... I might not have been in possession of all my faculties last night, and I was deeply in my cups, but... but I don't make animalistic sounds when I come, and I would never leave a woman unsatisfied."

She squinted at him, her nose twitching adorably. "What are you talking about?"

"What are *you* talking about?"

"I am talking about last night!"

"Well, so am I. And whenever I spend a passionate night in a woman's arms, whether it's her first time or not, I make certain to pleasure her before finding my own bliss."

"A passionate night?" She pursed her lips as if not to laugh. "Is that how you remember it?"

He crossed his arms over his chest. "How do *you* remember it?"

She licked her lips. "I remember you coming to my bed in the middle of the night. You appeared before me for the first time since you abandoned me right after we spoke our vows wearing a bouquet of odors I'd rather not remember. And the only bliss you found, lucky for me, was that of a deep slumber."

"Slumber?"

"Yes! You undid your breeches and fell on top of me! I could barely breathe, and it took me half the night to slide from beneath you only for you to shift and force me off the bed! I slept—or attempted to sleep—on the settee. And the moment I drifted into sleep, I'd wake up from your loud and obnoxious snoring!"

"I resent the implication that I was not able to perform my marital duty!" Perhaps it wasn't the part he should've concentrated on, but it was a matter of pride.

She let out a laugh of disbelief. "You resent the truth?"

He started undoing the falls of his breeches again. "Fine. Then we shall do it right here. Now."

She took a step back, her face a picture of obstinance. "I'd rather die."

He paused with his hands on the band of his breeches. "I might not remember most of last night, but I do remember you vowing to obey me."

"And I also remember our deal." She didn't miss a beat. "I conceded to not interfere in your affairs as long as it did not affect me, but *this* does. I am not going to be treated like a trollop. And you are not to come to my bedchamber unless you are completely sober."

Tyrone scoffed, watching his new bride carefully. If this was how she wanted to play it, so be it. But he was going to win. "Then I won't grace your bed at all," he said with a deceptive softness. "However, keep in mind that until we consummate our marriage, you are not officially my bride. Which means..." His pause was deliberate, his eyes condescendingly running down her body. "That you don't get any allowance."

Then he turned on his heels and stalked away.

The blood still boiled in his veins and the colors around him became vibrant somehow. This dull, dusty house full of nasty memories only ever livened up for him when he was drunk.

Drunk. Hmm.

What a glorious idea.

Chapter Eight

Her husband held his promise. Ever since their confrontation in her bedroom the morning after their nuptials, he hadn't come to her bed, nor did he arrange for her allowance. In fact, he hadn't appeared in the house at all.

Emily regretted her behavior. Why oh why hadn't she lied during the conversation with the duke? One little lie could have solved all of her problems. At the very least, she shouldn't have barred him from her chamber. She had turned their fight over and over in her mind, rewriting the dialog, changing her answers. But, of course, the best ideas came after the fact. At that moment, she had felt sickly, tired, and lacking sleep. She couldn't have acted more rationally.

However, his absence allowed Emily to settle her family into the townhouse without his interference. Two days later, she decided to take her family for a jaunt in the park.

The day was truly beautiful. The sun shone above their heads, the birds chirped their cheerful songs, and the fresh air was a welcome change to the stale and dull atmosphere of the Tyrone townhouse.

Reggie, dressed up like a little gentleman, walked up front, looking around the park in awe as if he'd never seen the place.

Harriet and Sophie walked arm in arm, unashamedly studying the gowns of every passing lady, giggling and dreaming up the perfect gowns they'd wear to their come-out balls.

Emily hoped she could patch things up with her duke before that time came. Harriet was seventeen, old enough for her debut. But considering the scandal surrounding Emily, she thought it was better to wait a year. She hoped she would find enough friends among the *ton* in that time to make her sister's debut smoother.

Her husband could've made her entry into society easier. But of course, the reprobate was more interested in spending his nights in an inebriated stupor.

She wasn't a saint in this marriage, either. Their last conversation proved as much.

She had never let emotions take over her logic before. For some reason, her husband brought out the worst qualities in her... Or at least, he brought out a range of emotions she didn't think she was capable of exhibiting.

She took a deep breath, thankful to be walking in silence by her mother's side as she sorted through her feelings.

There were so many things she wanted to tell her mother—so many burdens she wanted to lay upon her mother's shoulders. She'd married to solve all her problems, but the problems proved to be obstinate in that regard.

A few minutes into their walk, Emily started noticing something strange.

Some passersby paid undue attention to their little family. Women covered their faces with their fans and bowed their heads toward their companions whispering something while not taking their eyes off Emily.

Was it because they were wearing old-fashioned and slightly worn clothing? Perhaps her hair peeked out of her bonnet?

Emily brought a hand to her short locks when she heard one of the ladies say something to her companion that cleared everything up.

"Is this the duke's mistress?" she asked. "Oh, yes, I am sure she is! I saw them frolicking that day on Petticoat Lane!"

Emily's eyes widened, her cheeks burning from embarrassment. Was that what everyone was talking about?

She only hoped her mother didn't hear the conversation.

"I heard they're married now," another lady chimed in.

"I doubt it. He would've introduced her into society," the first lady continued, quite loudly.

"Can you blame him? Look at the rags she's wearing. He is probably ashamed of her."

Emily's heart racing, she hurried her steps. Her mother weaved her arm through hers and forced her to slow down. "Don't let them know they hurt you."

Emily swallowed as the hope that her mother had not heard the conversation died in her chest.

Still, she raised her head high and continued walking.

But she could no longer ignore the snickers, the whispers, and the sidelong glances. Now she knew what the *ton* was talking about. *Her.*

Duchess or not, her reputation was in tatters.

Every problem she had hoped to solve by marrying the duke still loomed ominously over her head.

Harriett and Sophie paused and looked back at Emily, their eyes full of hurt and glistening with tears.

They'd heard it, too.

It was too much. Emily wanted to run away, hide from the world and the judgmental gazes, and never come out. But her mother patted her hand, silently encouraging her to stay strong. If not for herself, then for her siblings.

Emily prayed they'd finish the walk with their dignity intact. And then she would... What would she do?

She couldn't do anything. Those people were right.

The duke hadn't even acknowledged her as his wife. He'd taken away her allowance. She was living under his roof like a beggar and she looked like it too.

Fury and shame burned inside her, traveling from the tip of her toes to the top of her head. She felt the spark of anger that was threatening to ignite.

She was not angry with these people, who judged her without knowing her. No. She was angry at her reprobate of a husband who let this happen. Who left her all alone and unprotected while drinking himself into oblivion.

And then things got even worse.

A few feet away, she noticed the O'Malley family walking toward them. In the first row, Astrid walked, her arm entwined with her mother's, and a few discrete paces away was Bernard with a beautiful young lady on his arm.

Something stuck inside Emily's throat resembling a large boulder, obstructing her breathing. Her face burned even more, scalding her cheeks and drying her mouth. She couldn't feel her legs, or any of her limbs really—it was a miracle she managed to move at all.

She turned toward Astrid and directed her a wobbly smile, ready to greet the woman, except at that exact moment, Mrs. O'Malley pointedly turned away, shielding her daughter and openly cutting Emily in front of the park full of people. "Some people should learn," she proclaimed loudly as they passed Emily, "that it requires a lot more to be a duchess than just marrying a title."

Emily swallowed hard. Her eyes burned with tears and she bit her lip painfully to keep from crying out. Her lost gaze met Bernard's and for a moment, she thought she'd found solace.

They were friends. They used to be in love. He cared about her, she knew.

But instead of support or encouragement, he took a cue from his mother and pointedly turned away.

Emily was ready to pick up her skirts and scamper away right then and there. She'd be happier if the earth opened up and swallowed her whole. But her mother tightened her grip on her and spoke through her feigned smile. "Just keep walking, darling. Don't give them more reasons to gossip. You did nothing wrong."

Emily swallowed hard, forcing herself to breathe again.

No, I've done everything wrong.

Chapter Nine

The dimly lit tavern was ablaze with vibrant colors and sparkling lights, casting a glittering haze over everything in sight. Tyrone picked up a glass of whisky and tossed it down his throat. The lively music was like a symphony of pure bliss and joy, each note resonating within him and filling him with inexplicable delight.

"Let's dance!" He tugged on the arm of a bar wench and spun her onto the dance floor.

The people around him became dazzling figures, their movements as graceful as swans. The women in their flowing dresses and shining hair seemed otherworldly, and his friends were like jovial giants, booming laughter and jokes that seemed to fill the entire room.

In this dreamlike state, Tyrone felt like he was on top of the world. All his worries and troubles had vanished, leaving him with nothing but pure, unadulterated joy.

The world was spinning around him, the lights flickering and the people's faces blurring into one. He didn't care. He was lost in the magic of the moment, a child again, free of all the weight and worries of adulthood. He could feel the eyes of the women on him, admiring his charm and style, and it only added to his sense of elation.

For Tyrone, there was no sadness, no regret, no pain.

Someone tapped on his shoulder, and he turned around to a large, bald man, staring down at him from his great height.

"What's the matter, good sir?" Tyrone slurred.

"Get your hands off my wench, you toff!" he growled.

"Which wench?" Tyrone theatrically looked around. Then he snaked his arm around the woman's waist and brought her closer to his body. "Oh, this one?"

The next moment he was sitting on the floor, the area around his eye radiating pain. Someone rushed past him and tackled the giant who'd just threatened—quite possibly punched—Tyrone.

A sudden loud bang sounded as someone smashed a bottle on the floor. Chaos erupted as fists started flying and chairs were hurled across the room. Tyrone rolled to the side, then deftly got to his feet and punched some man in the face. He didn't care who he was punching, as long as he got a few shots in. He was caught up in the brawl, swinging his fists wildly at anyone who came too close. His blood boiled and a smile broke out on his face. In this state, Tyrone knew he was invincible. He was a king, surrounded by his loyal subjects, and everything was bright, shiny, and perfect.

He didn't quite notice how it happened, but before he knew it, he was thrown on his arse, polishing the cobblestones with his breeches. The cold air hit him like a slap in the face, sobering him up a little. But the exhilaration of the moment was still with him, and he knew he couldn't let the night end just yet.

He laughed loudly, looking at his friends who were lying beside him in a drunken heap, then waved a hand. "The night is still young, gentlemen. I know a place where we can find a few more bottles of whisky." He grinned with wild abandon.

A racket downstairs woke Emily up. She sat up, squinting in the dark, listening intently when a loud knock sounded at the door. Her doorknob rattled before Sophie flew into her room.

"Do you hear that?" she whispered, her eyes wild as she climbed frantically into Emily's bed.

"Yes." Emily's voice was hoarse from sleep. She cleared her throat.

"I tried waking Harriet, but that girl sleeps like a log," Sophie complained. "What is that noise?"

The sharp sound of shattering glass made Emily flinch. It was followed by loud masculine laughter. Either they were being robbed, rather brazenly, or a more likely scenario was that her husband was finally home.

The door opened once more and Reggie appeared on the threshold. "Emily," he whispered. "I am scared."

Emily threw back the covers and slid off the bed. "Get under the covers, Reggie, and don't be scared. I shall take care of this!"

She jolted toward the chair which held her dressing gown, moving instinctively in the dark room.

"Ow!" She hit her shin against the chair and cursed loudly.

Sophie didn't react to her sister uncharacteristically spewing obscenities. "Where are you going?"

Reggie moved past her and climbed onto the bed beside his sister.

"Light the candle, will you?" Emily said irritably, trying to fit her arms into the dressing gown. Sophie did as asked and Emily swiftly grabbed the candle. She was already halfway out the door when she remembered to shout to her siblings, "Don't leave this room!"

Emily flew down the stairs like a fury, her angry steps echoing in the dark hall. Her face was twisted in anger and her eyes burned with a fiery determination. As she reached the bottom of the stairs, Emily paused, her hands balled into fists at her sides, listening to where the sounds of raucous laughter were coming from. She moved toward the noise, her dressing gown brushing against the floor and swishing around her ankles.

The library. That's where all the noise was coming from, she realized rather quickly and her fury intensified. If he needed to drink inside the house, why did he pick the room her family enjoyed the most?

She threw open the door and paused at the horrendous display.

Her eyes rounded as she took in her surroundings. The room was dark, illuminated only by a single fireplace. Most of the scene was swallowed by darkness but what she saw was enough for anger to spill out of her fingertips. Men, strange men, were lying on the floor in a state of half-undress. The bottles of whisky or some other alcohol—Emily didn't know what exactly—were strewn about the room, some empty, some still had liquid in them and some were broken, with glass scattered everywhere.

And then there was her husband, lying across from the fireplace with a large-bosomed woman, whose breasts were about to pop from her much too-small bodice, dancing right in front of him, waving her skirts about in a rather scandalous manner.

Emily fisted her hands so hard her palms hurt from the nails biting into her flesh. "Get out!" she breathed in a furious whisper.

The woman stopped dancing and turned to look at her. A few men raised their heads, interrupted from their pleasant daze. Only her husband seemed not to notice her as he waved at his dancing companion to continue.

Emily stepped closer and took a deep breath. "I said, everyone, get out!" she screamed loudly.

The woman covered herself with her arms and backed away from the duke. The men scrambled to their feet.

"You can't kick us out," one man slurred, wobbling on his feet.

"I gather from her tone that she can," another one countered.

"But it's the duke's house," the first one continued his protest.

"Who is she?" the third man slurred.

"I am the duchess," Emily said loudly. "This is my house, and I shall be damned if I let you disgrace it with your drunken presence. My mother is in this house, my siblings! Now pick up your things and leave!"

"Rrrawr," one gentleman mimicked the roar of a feline. "You never said you married a tigress, Tyrone."

Tyrone was absolutely out of his wits. He stared at her without a speck of recognition. "That's my wife," he finally slurred.

Emily turned her angry gaze toward the strangers in her house and they scrambled to get up and collect their belongings. A couple of men tripped and fell before finally, they all filed out of the room.

Emily stalked toward the bellpull and pulled hard. "You're a disgrace to your title," she seethed between her teeth. "A disgrace to the entire male race. How can you act like a complete imbecile while your family suffers? While we are shunned by the *ton*. Yes! I am your family. And I have had enough of your—" She turned toward him only to realize that he was lying flat on the floor, his chest rising and falling in peaceful slumber.

The butler walked into the room then and looked around, seemingly nonchalant. Probably, because this wasn't the first time he'd seen this room and his master in their current state of dishabille.

"Please, ask the footmen to convey His Grace into his room," Emily bit out. "And then I want to see all the servants first thing in the morning. I have an important task for them."

Surprise flickered on the butler's unperturbed features for a moment. Then he bowed and left the room.

Chapter Ten

Tyrone reached out his arm in search of his trusty bottle of whisky, and instead, patted the soft mattress.

He was in bed.

Was he in his wife's bed again?

He peeked through his heavy-lidded eyes only to realize he was in his own chamber. He turned onto his stomach and surveyed the floor.

Where was his drink? Usually, he had at least three bottles of whisky in the vicinity—now there were none.

He wanted to lift himself up. Instead, he tumbled down, hitting his head in the process. Tyrone sat up, seeing stars before his eyes. He waited for his vision to return before getting up and swaying toward the servants' bell. He pulled it and in the meantime went to perform his morning ablutions. He was surprised to feel a considerable growth on his face. How long had he been out drinking? And why in the hell was he back home?

His valet stepped into the room. "Would you like a warm bath, sir? Or shall I attend to your morning shave? I could offer you a refreshing cup of steaming coffee to help you start the day invigorated."

He was rambling. Why was he rambling? Tyrone narrowed his eyes suspiciously. "Bring me a glass of whisky. Actually, bring me the entire bottle." He turned away, then paused and looked back at his valet as he didn't move a muscle.

"Did you not hear what I said?" Tyrone raised a brow.

The valet straightened, his eyes running around the room as he wrung his hands. "Unfortunately, there is no whisky in the house."

"Then bring me brandy. Or gin. Or rum. Whatever we have will do." Tyrone waved a careless hand.

Bergen shuffled from one foot to another before mumbling under his breath, "There's none of that either."

"What?" Tyrone roared. He immediately flinched from a sharp pang in his temples. "What did you say?"

The valet stepped back. "Th-there is no liquor of any kind in the house, sir."

Tyrone stepped toward him, his hands fisted at his sides. "How come?" he asked silkily, with a deceptive calmness.

"The d-duchess ordered us to get rid of it all this morning. There is not a drop left."

Tyrone narrowed his eyes, then turned on his heel, and stalked to the adjoining room door. He flew into his wife's chamber, almost fuming from anger.

Luckily, the subject of his rage was calmly standing before the mirror, arranging her hair. Tyrone stomped toward her and growled close to her face, "Where is my whisky, duchess?"

His wife turned to him with infuriating calm. "I ordered the servants to pour it all away."

Tyrone rocked back on his heels. He'd expected her to stutter like a simpering fool. Yet she observed him with a cool demeanor, her eyes glinting with challenge. She wasn't afraid of him at all. Then perhaps she *was* a fool. "I truly hope you're joking."

She crossed her arms over her chest. Ah, finally a defensive gesture. "I am not."

"Well, then, you're going to go out and buy me some."

She raised her chin and repeated with a stubborn precision, "I am not."

"You think you actually matter, do you?" he seethed. "You think you're here to run the estate, to make the decisions?"

She didn't even flinch. The imp had grown into her role as a duchess overnight. "Someone has to."

Tyrone's lip twitched. That cut. Deeper than he'd thought it would. "I run this dukedom the way it deserves," Tyrone crooned. "I have been doing it for months."

"Truly?" she scoffed. "Because this townhouse is falling apart. The servants have been left to their own devices. There is barely any food in the cupboards. And if the way you treat this townhouse is any indication, I would say that your estates have not been taken care of since you became the duke while all you do is drink yourself into oblivion!"

"That is exactly what this dukedom deserves!" Tyrone gritted through his teeth then turned away and stalked toward the adjoining room door.

"You ruined my life!" she cried after him. "And by God, I am going to ruin yours in return."

He stopped in his tracks and turned toward her with a smirk on his lips. "That cretin Hawkridge was right, you are a tigress. Only there is nothing left to ruin, *mo tíogar.* And if you think that getting rid of spirits will make me sober, you better think again. Because I can drink elsewhere just as well."

"Wouldn't that be a blessing," she countered. Then, her voice rising with every word, she cried, "At least, this way, this house will be clean from the smell of foul drunken men and your cheap harlots!"

Heat crept up her neck and settled at the crests of her cheeks. Tyrone narrowed his eyes, his gaze dropping to her lips, his voice silky. "Ah! Is that what this was all about? You got rid of all the alcohol in the house to get me into bed with you?"

"What?" Her voice was a breathy whisper.

"You said to not grace your bed while I am drunk, but now you practically ensured my sobriety." He reached for his shirt buttons and started undoing them.

She took two steps back, her dark brown eyes frantic as he freed his shirt from his breeches and threw it over his head. He advanced toward his wife, like a panther stalking his prey.

"If that's what you wanted, all you had to do was ask."

"I think you should leave," she breathed out.

She took another step and her back hit the wall. She was trapped between him and the wall, her chest rising and falling with frantic breaths. Tyrone slapped his hands on either side of her head, caging her with his body.

"No, *mo tíogar*," he whispered in her ear as he leaned closer and had the satisfaction of seeing goosebumps run across her skin. "I think it is time we made it official. It is time I made you my wife."

His face descended on hers and in a moment, he caught her lips between his. She stood, unmoving, as he kissed her with unreserved ardor.

He wanted to frighten her. He wanted to show her that he was the master in the house and she was a mere guest. A nobody. She was to obey him.

But the sweet taste of her lips quickly eclipsed all his other thoughts and feelings. He turned into a rabid animal with the only salvation the lips of the woman before him. He lowered his hands and snaked his arms around her waist, bringing her aflush with his body.

She gasped and Tyrone took the opportunity to slip his tongue inside her wet crevice. Tyrone teased her with his tongue, tickling her, playing with her, exploring the corners of her mouth, and tasting her lovely, sweet flavor. Instead of drawing away, her hands shyly touched his chest and traveled up, heightening the burning sensations inside him.

She didn't even kiss him back. She just touched him lightly, let out a breathy moan, and that was enough for Tyrone to lose his head. His one hand traveled to her neck while the other still held her by the waist. His fingers tangled in her hair, removing the pins she'd meticulously placed just a moment ago, and tugged on her —short?—locks. She sighed, the sound reverberating through his entire body. Her head fell back and Tyrone released her lips, peppering kisses along her jaw, her neck, and lower still.

What am I doing?

Tyrone paused before his lips touched the soft mounds over her bodice, his warm breath hitting against her skin and chasing the gooseflesh along her chest. He closed his eyes, forcing himself to stop this madness, and stepped away.

She swayed and had to catch his arm to steady herself.

Her breathing was frantic, her eyes wild, her short hair mussed. She was gorgeous like that. Her lips were swollen from his kisses, her cheeks red from passion, her eyes glowing. She licked her lips and his gaze followed the motion. He wanted to kiss her again.

What madness was that?

He looked into her brown eyes, brilliant with unshed tears, and saw the entire world reflected in them—the world that was full of color again, the way it was when he was drunk. And perhaps he *was* drunk, just not on alcohol, but on the woman standing before him.

He didn't want her to know how off-balance he felt just then. And luckily, she seemed just as disoriented as he.

So, he took a deep breath and gave a sharp nod. "I hope you learned your lesson."

Chapter Eleven

E mily sat at the dinner table later that evening, surrounded by the comforting chatter of her family, yet she struggled to focus on the conversation. Her mind kept drifting back to her husband and their morning encounter in his bedchamber.

She blinked, attempting to regain her focus, but it quickly drifted to the dreamland where her husband held her tightly to the hot and hard plains of his body as his tongue probed her mouth with a firm but tender insistence.

What was it about his kiss that made her a slave to these thoughts?

She'd been kissed before. Multiple times. And not a single kiss had felt like this animalistic ravagement. She wasn't even sure she could call that onslaught of his lips, tongue, and teeth a kiss.

He'd wanted to humiliate her. To bend her into submission. And for one short moment, he'd succeeded.

Apparently, that was all that he'd needed.

And for some unfathomable reason, Emily could not get that abomination of a kiss out of her mind. The memory of his mouth on hers still made her lips tingle and her body tremble.

Perhaps, it was merely confusion. Because she had never, not in her wildest dreams, imagined that she would find his embrace pleasurable.

How could she?

She loathed the man.

Perhaps, it was because his kiss was so different from the ones she'd experienced before. Bernard's kisses had been more timid, almost uncertain, even during their most intimate moments... She wrinkled her nose. No, she would not think of Bernard. He deserved no more space in her head or her heart.

Did Tyrone?

She downcast her eyes, concentrating on chasing her food around the plate with a fork.

A part of her had thought that their kiss was a sign of new beginnings, that her husband would finally treat her as his wife.

She had been wrong.

He had not shown his face since then and he hadn't bothered to join the family for dinner, although she was certain he was still in the house.

"Maybe we should go home," Harriet said and that finally pulled Emily out of her thoughts.

"Home?" she asked. "You want to leave?"

Harriet shrugged. "Let's be honest, we are not welcome here. Not in this house and certainly not among the *ton*."

"So, you want to leave me here alone?" Emily asked, panic rising inside her chest.

Their mother took Emily's hand in hers and squeezed. "We are not going to leave you, dear. Not until you're ready."

"We are not helping, Emily," Harriet insisted. "You are only splitting your focus. Perhaps without us, you have a better chance to make yourself comfortable here, gain the trust of the servants, and maybe even bond with the duke."

"I don't want to go home," Sophie chimed in. "Have you not

seen the library in this place? Our entire house could fit in it. Twice."

"And Emily promised to find me a tutor," Reggie chimed in. "Or perhaps the duke can teach me—"

Emily scoffed. "The duke has no knowledge to impart about anything."

"So, you agree with Harry? You want us to leave?" Reggie's eyes were wide and his lower lip trembled. Despite the fact that Emily had promised her sisters an entry into the *ton*, a debut, new clothes, and prospects, Reggie was the one who was most excited about staying in London.

Perhaps he hoped to finally find someone who would help him grow into his role as the man of the house, a baronet, worthy of his title. He had been too young when they lost their father, and their guardian was nothing but a disappointment.

And now, there was a new man in his life—his sister's husband. And that man was bound to disappoint him, too.

Perhaps Harriet was right, and it was better if they went home.

Except that Emily didn't even have enough funds to send them on their way. At least this house had food.

"No, of course not. But I wouldn't rely on the duke for anything. If he can't even be bothered to show up for dinner—"

Of course, right at that moment, loud steps echoed through the corridor, the doors were thrown open, and the duke appeared on the threshold.

Emily wasn't prepared to see him and she was prepared even less for the flush that covered her skin at the sight of him.

Her family shot from their chairs and dipped into curtsies and bows, as the duke, with a waistcoat hanging open, his hair disheveled, stomped toward the table. He didn't bother to utter a greeting or even look at anyone except for Emily. And Emily was grateful for that, because the look in his eyes was anything but pleasant. "Why wasn't I informed that we had company?" he growled.

She fisted her fingers by her sides and stood. "This is my family. I am certain you remember my mother, Mrs. Fitzwilliam."

"Good evening, Your Grace," her mother said, but Tyrone wasn't paying attention. Instead, he leaned over the table and reached for the bottle of wine sitting in the middle. His hand was shaking, and a bead of sweat ran down his forehead.

"My sisters Harriet, Sophie, and—"

Without letting Emily finish, he turned on his heel and stomped away.

There was a beat of silence as everyone around the table tried to process what had just happened until Sophie finally broke the silence. "I think I liked Bernard more."

Emily tried for a polite smile before wiping her hands on the napkin and rounding the table. "Excuse me," she mumbled under her breath as she left the room.

Emily flew through the house, entering the duke's chamber on his heels.

He turned, a glimmer of surprise flickering in his eyes. "What do you want?" he barked.

"What do *I* want?" she seethed. "I want the world to stop treating my family with disdain. What do *you* want? Because if you want to be rude to me, that's just fine. Perhaps, I deserve it. Perhaps, I should have expected it. But please, spare my family from your brutish behavior. They did nothing to earn your contempt and be the laughingstock of the *ton*!"

"This is my house," he growled over her last few words, waving his hand in the air. It was shaking. *He* was shaking. "They are unwanted guests, and I can act around them any way I please!"

He stomped toward his bedside table and carefully sat down the bottle of wine he'd so unceremoniously snatched from their table. His back was to her, but she could feel the tension in his posture.

"What is wrong with you?" she asked with genuine curiosity. For the first time, she wondered if his behavior had nothing to do with her, nor did it have anything to do with her family. There were other demons he was battling. His own.

"What is wrong with me?" He scoffed and turned toward her. "*You* are what's wrong with me! You barged into my life and turned it upside down. Forced me to marry you—"

"I didn't force anything. You tracked me down, remember?"

"—poured away all my liquor, brought your chattering family under my roof, and you want me to be polite about it?"

"Yes!" she snapped. "I want you to act like a proper duke."

He scoffed. "A duke. Of course."

"Yes, a duke. That's what you are. Why is it so difficult for you to accept? You keep asking what I want as if I am asking for something unattainable. What I want is basic respect toward my family and courtesy toward me as your wife. I am willing to do anything in order to be a perfect duchess. All I need from you is to be a duke. A man who cares for his lands and his family. I want to be a proper mistress, hostess, and wife, and to give you heirs. And I can be all that, if only you weren't standing in my way."

"Did you ever think there is a reason for that?" He took a slow step forward like a predator. "I don't need a perfect duchess. I need you to stay away from my affairs."

"You don't need a duchess? If you're content with the poor way your household is managed, and you have no need for me, then why marry me at all?"

He grimaced and ran both his hands through his hair. "I had my reasons, however ill-advised."

Emily stepped back, her hands fisted by her sides, her face hot. "You are a beast."

"And you'd do well to remember that," he whispered menacingly. "It is best you leave now, Duchess."

"No!" She raised a finger in warning. "If you don't need a proper duchess, I have no need to pretend to be meek now, do I?"

"When have you *ever* been meek?" he asked with a swipe of his hand through the air.

"You refuse to show me respect, you refuse to share my bed, then guess what? I shall find someone else to fulfill those needs!"

There. She was letting her emotions get the better of her again. He wasn't the only one who could dole out idle threats. She just wished that he cared enough for her words to hurt him.

She turned on her heel, her hands shaking, her breaths heaving out of her chest. But before she could reach the door handle, she was turned around in a whirlwind of heat and strength and trapped between the door and two hundred pounds of raw, angry male.

"Try it," he snarled, his face so close to hers that his warm breath hit her cheek. "Any man who tries to so much as touch you will regret it before he succeeds."

Well, she'd gotten her wish.

"I refuse to be disrespected in this marriage," she breathed. "And if you don't provide me with—"

He cut her off with a rough kiss on her lips. "Is this what you want?" he whispered between kisses. One arm propped against the door, the other snaked around her waist, tightening the fabric of her gown, bunching it in his fist. "Is this the kind of respect you are looking for, *mo tíogar*?"

Emily knew he was trying to intimidate her again. To push her away.

Why was he trying so hard to keep her at a distance?

Her mind refused to dissect the possible reasons; it refused to work altogether. Because despite his attempts to frighten her, Emily was drawn to him instead.

What madness was this?

The heat of his body beckoned her to him, the pressure of his lips invited her to pull him closer, to learn his taste.

Emily arched her back, pressing her breasts against his chest, savoring the feel of his hard body against hers. Her hands glided up his arms, one hand curled around the nape of his neck, her fingers delving into his thick locks, drawing him closer.

Tyrone growled, taking a step closer, pinning her against the door as he hoisted her higher, until her feet dangled in the air, his pelvis rubbing against her center.

Emily gasped, and he took advantage, slipping his tongue inside and sweeping it proprietarily over her mouth.

Emily held him tighter, one of her legs hiking up to hook her knee over his thigh, trying to hold on to this man like he was a lifeline. Sensations were firing inside her one after another, not knowing which touch or which sound aroused the heat within her. She touched her tongue to his, craving to know his taste, and he groaned into her mouth.

That animalistic sound told her that he was as lost in passion as she was.

He thrust his pelvis, and she could feel his cock, hot and hard pressing against her center even through the skirts of her gown and his breeches.

Suddenly she wished there was no fabric separating their bodies. She wanted to feel his skin against hers, feel his hardness against her soft curves. Feel him... inside her.

He tore his mouth away and pressed his forehead against hers, his breathing labored. "Is this what you deserve? Is this how you deserve to be treated?" he whispered, then disengaged her hands from his neck and took a step back. "Like a trollop."

Emily's feet hit the floor, roughly and unceremoniously dropping her back into the unpleasant reality. The heat of her husband's body left her, and she was alone again, cold, and confused.

"And if you think I shall bed you for the sake of having heirs, then think again," he growled as he turned away. "I refuse to have a hand at continuing the Tyrone line. I'll die first. Now get out."

Standing with his back to her, against the light of the raging fire, his hair mussed, his body tensed, now, he truly looked like a beast.

With a shaking hand, Emily found the door handle, turned it, and fled into the sanctuary of her own room, pressing her back against the wall.

Tears burned at the back of her eyes, and her stomach churned. She pressed her hand against her belly, as it was rising and falling with her shallow breaths.

Is this how you deserve to be treated?

And for the first time in a long time, Emily believed that perhaps she did.

Like a trollop.

Because she had indeed acted like one. No, not today. Earlier. Way earlier, before she had even met Tyrone.

She pushed off the wall, slowly glided to her dressing room, and walked inside.

She picked up the little metal container from the corner where she'd hidden it a few days ago.

I refuse to have a hand in continuing the Tyrone line. I'll die first.

There was a chance he would not have a choice in the matter. Because if her fears proved to be true—

She opened the lid of the container and stared at the little green shoots.

The barley seeds had sprouted.

Which meant only one thing. Her fears were indeed justified.

She was definitely with child.

Chapter Twelve

Tyrone's hand was shaking.

His entire body was, but his hand was what he concentrated on at the moment.

He loathed himself for the way he'd treated his wife just now. She didn't deserve it.

Nobody deserved it. But he had no choice.

His mood was foul, he wasn't in full control of his faculties, his head was aching, and his mind was nagging at him to go get a bottle of whisky.

He prowled toward his side table, took the bottle of wine in his hand, and tightened his fingers around it until his knuckles grew white.

With a roar, he tossed the bottle into the fire, suddenly feeling a little better.

It was like a weight had been lifted off his shoulders.

He knew himself quite well. He was often in a foul and aggressive mood when he was getting over the effects of long alcohol use. He had to frighten his wife away because he didn't want to inadvertently hurt her.

He would never raise a hand to her, just the thought made

him nauseous. Rather he was afraid he would hurt her in his throes of passion.

Just now, having her in his arms, as she was innocently returning his kisses, all he could think of was tossing up her skirts and burying himself so deep inside her that he wouldn't know where he ended and she began.

He didn't want to wait. He didn't want to prepare her, pleasure her, or comfort her. All he wanted was to alleviate his beastly needs. And while he was in this mood, it was best she wasn't around him at all.

Better she thought of him as a beast than become the beast in truth.

He fisted his hands by his side, forcing himself to calm down.

But he couldn't. Her scent still lingered in the room, her taste lingered on his lips, and he could feel her as if she was still in his arms.

So soft, so pliant, so wonderfully giving.

Even when he had been ravaging her like a wild animal, she'd welcomed him into her arms and kissed him back... gently.

Tyrone undid the falls of his breeches and took himself in hand. He was hard and aching. For her.

Now, all alone, with his wife safely tucked away in her room, he could finish what he had started.

He could imagine doing exactly what he wanted to do to her without the fear of hurting her.

He slid his hand up and down his shaft, as the images of his wife flickered before his eyes. She was standing before him, taking off that shabby day gown, pressing her body against his, and running her hands all over him.

He remembered her sweet kisses and imagined ravaging her mouth with all his ardor. Suddenly she was on her knees before him, the innocent look in her gaze turned tantalizing as she encircled his cock with her soft hand and then licked the tip before sucking in the head of his cock.

Tyrone pumped his shaft, his hips moving in a passionate rhythm, as he imagined fucking her sweet little mouth. And of course, in his mind, in his thoughts, she enjoyed it.

She urged him on with her sultry gaze and her throaty whimpers, all the while working miracles with her tongue.

Two more thrusts and Tyrone spilled himself over his fist, the foggy image of his wife on her knees disappearing before him.

God, he wanted her.

He still wanted her.

But he didn't deserve her.

Emily padded down the long corridor and knocked on the door of the only person who could advise her on what to do, the only person who would not judge her and would help her during this tumultuous time. The person she wished she didn't have to bother, but the only person who could comfort her at a moment like this.

The door creaked, and her mother's dear but pale face appeared from within. Right at that moment, Emily's face crumbled and she broke into tears.

Mother's arms embraced her immediately, her comforting scent enveloping Emily, her warmth, her softness like a balm to Emily's battered soul. Emily didn't know how long she cried in her mother's embrace; she didn't even realize when they'd moved to the little settee by the hearth or when she wiped away her tears and took her mother's hands. But as that happened, Emily looked up at her mother and confessed, "Mother, I am with child."

Her mother's eyes widened for a moment before she looked away. When she turned back, she was biting on her lower lip, her face scrunched in a little grimace. "It's Bernard's, isn't it?"

Emily nodded, a little hiccup escaping her lips as she wiped away more tears.

"How long?"

Emily licked her lips. "Eight or nine weeks."

"And your husband doesn't know? No," she continued as Emily shook her head. "Of course not."

"Mother, I am so embarrassed. And Father would be so ashamed of me! I got with child out of wedlock and then tricked another man to marry me..." A hiccup. She wiped her tears away, her body shaking. "How must you be disappointed."

Her mother shook her head. "I am not, dear. Look at me." She gently cupped Emily's cheek, her gaze tender. "I could never be disappointed in you."

"But I acted irresponsibly."

Her mother smiled gently. "You did, that is true. But you loved Bernard and you believed that he loved you too. You would not be the first person ever to have relations out of wedlock. In fact, your father and I... we also anticipated our vows."

Emily paused, her anguish interrupted by shock as she stared at her blushing mother. "You did?"

"Dear, you were born in January. Your father and I married in July, how do you think that worked?" Strangely, Emily had never once thought about it. "Those who are without sin, let them first cast a stone. The only difference between you and me is that your father was an honorable man. He married me and saved us—you and me—from ruin. Bernard did not. And what you did next, you did out of necessity, out of care and love for your siblings. You acted out of love both times. And I would never condemn you for that."

"But what do I do now?" Emily whispered. "How do I tell my husband?"

Her mother chewed her lower lip in thought. "Have you... Did you... Is your marriage consummated?"

Emily shook her head.

"Right." Her mother frowned, looking into the fire as her

thumbs absently stroked Emily's knuckles. An oddly comforting gesture. "Well, you need to."

Emily reeled back. "You mean I have to pretend the child is his?" This was the last thing she expected her mother to say.

"Emily, I would never advise you to trick anybody. But you've seen your husband. He is angry, like a beast. I've heard rumors about his father. He was ruthless. And if the apple doesn't fall far from the tree, can you imagine what the duke will do to you when he finds out the truth about the babe? You need to make certain he thinks it's his."

Emily took a moment to process the words before saying, "But the timeline won't fit! He will find out!"

"Not necessarily. He doesn't seem very interested in your affairs. After the season is over, you can retreat home with us. Tell him that you're more comfortable spending your confinement with your family. Or you can go to a distant estate away from him. He does not need to know exactly when the child is born. He shan't take an interest in the babe beyond knowing its sex until the child is of age to go to school. And only if it's a boy. That's how little most noblemen care about their offspring. And from what I've seen of your husband..." She paused with a slight grimace. "He might care even less."

Emily swallowed. "You want me to carry out a life-long deceit?"

Her mother squeezed her fingers. "You did your duty to us as your family; you saved us from poverty and ruin. Now it is time to protect your unborn child."

Chapter Thirteen

Tyrone stared at his clean-shaven face in the looking glass. His eyes were sullen, his cheeks sunken, and his skin was pale.

He glanced at the hearth, where the broken pieces of a wine bottle still lay at the edge, and let out a deep sigh. He had been drinking for weeks, ever since he returned to British soil. And his appearance and his grim mood were the result of that drinking.

He knew himself well. Everything was bright and colorful when he was drunk, but the moments right after were hell. And for the first time in weeks, he was ready to go through hell in order to come out on the other side even if he didn't know what awaited him there. He wasn't quite certain why he wanted it, either.

It had something to do with last night. Something to do with the look in his wife's eyes...

He shook off the memory, then quickly got dressed and made his way downstairs.

Light chatter and laughter came from behind the closed doors of the breakfast room, making him pause. It was so unusual to hear sounds of joy in this house, so foreign. He lingered behind the closed doors, listening, and a small smile appeared on his face.

But the moment he opened the door and entered the breakfast room, the chattering stopped. It was as if the warmth was sucked out of the room, replaced by the chill surrounding him.

Tyrone paused in the awkward silence before making his way to the head of the table. The women slowly slid from their chairs to curtsy, but Tyrone's eyes were on his wife, who remained seated.

There was something different about her. Was it her hair? It wasn't pinned as usual, and for that he was grateful. He despised her sleek look. What surprised him though, was the length—or should he say shortness—of her hair. It suited her.

Her short locks only accentuated her round brown eyes, her full, rosy lips, and her pronounced cheekbones.

She met his gaze and her cheeks reddened, adding a vibrant flush to her already radiant face. Her lips grew darker somehow, her eyes brighter and even the room around her became awash with color.

Perhaps, it was just a trick of the light—a wayward ray of sun sifting through the heavy morning clouds.

The scrape of the chair caught his attention and Tyrone turned toward a little boy, about ten years old, as he bowed toward him before returning to his seat.

He didn't look Tyrone in the eyes as he did so, and he didn't look at him now with his eyes glued to his plate, his fork tightly clenched between his shaking fingers.

The boy was afraid of him.

Something twisted in Tyrone's gut, and he tore his eyes away. He looked around the table and was met by curious glances, some shy, others more brazen. At least, not everyone was terrified of him it seemed.

His gaze returned to the boy who still refused to meet his gaze.

Look me in the eye when I enter the room! A gentleman doesn't hide his gaze, you useless mutt! His father's words rang in his ears.

"How lovely of you to join us," his wife said, pulling him out of his dreadful memories. "I was starting to worry we wouldn't see you till the end of the season."

"Were you?" he asked roughly. "Or were you perhaps worried that you would?"

She met his gaze steadily. "You are the master of this house. It is always an honor to be in your presence."

She was so proper, so polite, not giving away a hint of her true feelings. She wore this polite mask well. But it only amused him. He'd seen her unmasked the night before. He'd tasted her passion.

"Is it?" He narrowed his eyes and lowered them to her lips, before meeting her gaze again. "Even when I act like a beast?"

Her cheeks flushed further, her lips trembling, as her icy exterior began to crumble. Was she remembering their kiss, too?

She took a deep breath and answered without breaking eye contact, "I was hoping to finally meet the man beneath the beastly facade."

Tyrone held his wife's gaze. He saw a challenge in it. Was she daring him to shed his facade right now? Or was she wondering if he was even capable of it at all? Neither of those questions were the ones she should have been worried about. The real question was whether the human beneath his facade was any better than the beast.

A clearing of the throat broke the spell between them and his wife looked away.

"We wanted to thank you," her mother said, "for welcoming us into your home."

Tyrone popped a piece of food into his mouth and answered around a bite, "Your daughter didn't give me a choice."

His wife visibly tensed, her fingers whitening from the pressure applied to her fork. But her mother didn't seem perturbed or offended by his words.

"Then, perhaps, I should thank you for taking my daughter as your wife and making her the mistress of your home," she said in a soft but firm voice.

"Yes," Tyrone said, concentrating his gaze on the older woman. She didn't emit the kind of radiance that her daughter did. She was frail with ghostly white skin, but he could see the familial resemblance clearly. He could see his wife in her, and he wondered how alike they were in other aspects. "You must be so happy that your daughter has landed a duke."

He felt his wife's dagger-like gaze even if he wasn't looking at her. She was about to say something, probably something scathing, but her mother answered in the same soft voice, unbothered by the implication in his question, "I am grateful to you for saving us from disgrace. Unfortunately, our society puts much value on such things as reputations and outward appearances. One little misstep can cause a great deal of pain when instead, one should be paying attention to one's character. My daughter is hard-working, clever, selfless, and kind. And I do hope that you shall judge her based upon that, and not on the fact that in a moment of hardship, she did what she had to do and relied upon your generosity. If you do that, and you and my daughter learn to live in harmony, I will, in fact, be very happy."

Tyrone studied the woman with narrowed eyes, yet saw nothing but sincerity on her face. Or perhaps she was an accomplished liar.

"Your daughter," he said slowly, "poured away all my whisky."

Her mother finished chewing unhurriedly before answering. "I am certain she had a good reason."

Tyrone couldn't help the chuckle that left his lips. He noticed that his wife relaxed her grip on the fork, too.

"I am beginning to see the resemblance between you two," he said, looking from mother to daughter. *More than in appearance.* Then he shrugged in his carefree manner as he poked at his food. "I mean that as a compliment."

His wife flicked a glance at him that said, *I doubt it,* and he flashed her a smile.

The atmosphere lightened around the table. His wife turned to one of her sisters and asked something about a piano piece she was working on. Tyrone didn't listen for the specifics. He just enjoyed the comforting buzz of conversation floating about the table and watched his wife and her siblings tease each other back and forth about their musical talents or lack thereof.

Tyrone watched his wife, his chest filling with warmth with her every smile, butterflies fluttering in his stomach when he heard her laugh.

She was beautiful.

He remembered the first time he saw her quite vividly. And he couldn't figure out how he had found her plain at that moment. As he watched the animated features of her face, her radiant smile and glittering eyes that shone like diamonds, the short, wavy hair that bounced with her every movement, he couldn't see her as anything but gorgeous.

She glanced at him then, a questioning look in her eyes. He'd been staring at her for a long time, he realized. Instead of hastily looking away, he raised a brow in challenge.

Her cheeks instantly reddened, and she shook her head at him as though he was a mischievous boy caught stealing sweets from the kitchen.

"I enjoyed the outing to the park," the boy said as Tyrone returned his attention to the table.

"Until we were cut," one of his sisters noted.

Cut?

"Perhaps we should go with the duke next time," the duchess offered, "so he can show his acceptance of us."

The table descended into silence for a short moment. They were waiting for his answer.

"I hate being on display," he answered distractedly. Were they cut? When was this? An uncomfortable ache settled in his chest.

"We should hold a musical then," the youngest sister said with a dose of sarcasm. "Then we will definitely be shunned by the *ton* for the rest of our lives."

The young boy quickly changed the subject and started talking about horses or races. Tyrone wasn't listening anymore.

He remembered his wife's earlier words about being treated with disdain. And how he, the idiot, had not paid any attention.

Why would he? In his drunken stupor and then the fog of early soberness, nothing mattered to him. But as he sat surrounded by the friendly and cheerful banter, he couldn't help but remember the silent, tension-filled dinners of his childhood. And he never wanted to be the reason this house was filled with tension ever again.

"We are going to the theater on the morrow," the duke announced from the threshold of the adjoining room that evening, making Emily jump.

Brushing her hair by the soothing, crackling fire, she hadn't noticed the door opening. She didn't even know the duke was in the house. He had left soon after breakfast, and she assumed he would stay away until the end of the night. Probably drinking.

Yet, here he was, as large as life, and as sober as she'd ever seen him. And all her attempts at calming herself had vanished at the first sound of his voice. Her brush slipped past her fingers and fell to the floor with a dull thud.

His gaze lingered on her hair, a strange glint in his eyes. Emily's hand self-consciously flew to caress the short locks curling by her ears. "Tomorrow?"

"Yes. You wanted us to go out as a family, did you not? So people would see that I acknowledge you as my wife."

Emily cocked her head to the side in surprise. She hadn't thought he'd paid attention to her words.

"I reserved a booth for tomorrow. All..." He paused as if working something out in his mind. "...five of us?"

Emily raised a brow. *Six.*

"Seven? It doesn't matter. The booth has enough seats to fit everyone."

"I don't think it is proper to bring children to the theater. And Harriet, although of appropriate age, is not out in society yet."

He shrugged. "How is the theater different from a walk in the park? I can't see a reason the entire family can't enjoy a show. Besides, I invited a few friends to accompany us, and they will be devastated if we show up alone."

The entire family. Emily's chest tightened and warmth traveled from her stomach up to her cheeks. It felt nice that he acknowledged her family as his. Even if he didn't know how many siblings she had. Then his last sentence finally registered in her mind and she grimaced. "A few friends? Surely not the ones I cursed out of this house a few days ago?"

Tyrone let out a bark of laughter. "Yes, that was a rather entertaining night. And yes, Lucien Drake, one of the gents from that night, is going to accompany us. But you have nothing to worry about. He rather admires your... pluck."

Emily doubted it.

It probably showed on her face, because he chuckled as he continued, "He said so himself. He also said that it was about time someone took me under their heel." A mischievous smile graced his lips, and Emily froze in shock. She didn't think that her husband, the angry beast who snarled and growled at everything, could be this... charming. He leaned his shoulder against the wall, crossing his arms over his chest, looking relaxed. Emily hadn't thought he could be relaxed, either. "Not that that's ever going to happen."

"Will the Earl of Sutton be there as well?" she asked before picking up her brush and running it through her hair, just so she had something to do other than sit and stare at her husband as he was studying her from under his hooded eyelids.

He looked different tonight, somehow. Clean-shaven, with his hair—longer than hers—cascading down to his shoulders, an ironed-out crisp white shirt under his waistcoat. His breeches sat snug around his muscled thighs. His body was relaxed, yet he was alert, as though he would spring at any moment if needed.

He looked... What was that word she was looking for? Ah, yes, sober.

And it made him dangerously appealing.

But the moment she mentioned Sutton, he tensed, his eyes narrowing. "I've invited him, yes. Why are you curious about him?"

Was that a note of jealousy in his tone? Surely not. She lifted one shoulder in a shrug. "He helped me in my time of need. I believe he is the only decent friend you have."

"Decent?" He bristled. "At least I didn't hide you away at my estate. And I'd say taking your entire family to the theater qualifies as rather decent."

Emily raised both brows. He *was* jealous.

This was her chance. If she was ever to lure him into her bed, this was the perfect opportunity. He was sober. He was in her room. And he was exhibiting signs of jealousy. Surely this was what he came for?

But how did one go about inviting one's husband into one's bed? She wasn't a virgin, but she wasn't savvy in the art of seduction either.

She pushed off the floor and tried to get up as slowly and gracefully as she could. But of course, in her agitation, she tripped over her nightgown and almost plummeted back to the floor.

She would have, if not for her husband. He pounced, and in one quick motion, he was right in front of her, his warm hands holding her by the shoulders. Emily let out a nervous laugh. "Thank you," she said as she straightened to her full height, shaking and burning from embarrassment. He still didn't let go of her. She swallowed. "And thank you for arranging the theater. It will mean the world to my family."

He absently caressed her upper arms with his thumbs, while his eyes bore straight into her soul. "I am just doing my duty as your husband."

His voice was dark and sensual. Butterflies fluttered in her stomach, her heart racing in her chest. If her husband dropped his gaze lower, she was certain he would see it pounding. She took a deep breath, inhaling the pleasant scent of his soap and his manly musk. And she was flooded by an inexplicable urge to bury her nose in his chest or neck, to feel more of him. Heat spread through her entire body and settled in her cheeks, her belly, and low between her legs. She licked her dry lips. "Duty, right." She raised her arm and ran a finger along the seam of his waistcoat. "Is that why you're here? To fulfill your marital duty?"

His eyes tracked the path of her finger before he raised his eyes to hers. They were dark and hooded, glinting with fire. "Are you trying to seduce me, Duchess?"

She knew she needed to seduce him. She needed him to believe the child inside her was his. But at this moment, as he looked at her as if she was the only woman on earth, as if he was ready to devour her, she couldn't think of it as a duty. She wanted to experience his kiss again. She wanted to experience his touch. Everywhere. The wanton thought almost knocked her back on her heels. Instead, she looked up at him. "Should I be?"

The duke raised his hand and slowly, sensually, touched her cheek with a tip of one finger. She had the urge to lean into his touch, to rub her face against his hand like a cat. He moved his finger lightly over her skin, sending prickling sensations down her body, tracing it all the way to her ear before tucking a lock of hair behind it. Emily's breath caught and her mouth went suddenly dry. Standing so close to him, feeling the heat emanating from him, reminded her of the time his lips were on her, wreaking havoc on her senses.

If he were to kiss her now, she wouldn't let him stop. She was no longer the seducer, but the seduced. She'd let him do anything he wished to do to her. And she was afraid she was going to enjoy every moment.

He leaned forward, until his mouth was only an inch away from hers, and whispered, "You should let your hair free more often." Then he straightened to his full height and smiled. "This short style is called A la Titus. It's all the rage in Paris."

Before Emily could decipher his words and collect her emotions, he was already gone, locking the door behind him with a decisive click.

Chapter Fourteen

She looked iridescent.

Her gown was faded and worn and her spencer-jacket was too threadbare, especially for a cold spring night, but even surrounded by the most fashionable ladies of the *ton,* she still stood out like a diamond among unassuming pebbles.

Her family was also dressed modestly in old-fashioned but neat clothing. And it took Tyrone a moment to realize that the reason they were dressed this way was that he had cut off her allowance and had forgotten to resume it. He'd been too preoccupied with his own issues, trying to delve into the estate matters and keep his mind from drinking that he hadn't paid attention to his wife and her struggles.

He paid attention to her now.

Her sweet flowery scent wafted toward him as they walked side by side, her warmth spreading through his right side and heating him from the inside out.

And she'd let her hair down.

He liked to think she did it in an attempt to please him, although it could have been that she'd finally realized that trying to pin it was a useless endeavor.

Her hand tightened on his arm as they weaved their way through the crowd, trying to ignore the appraising gazes unashamedly thrown her way.

She quietly stood beside him, as he stopped to introduce her to his acquaintances, not saying anything beyond a simple polite word and granting them an occasional timid smile. She was different from the woman he'd gotten to know—the tigress, who was ready to rip anyone to shreds with her bare teeth to defend her family, the woman who stood up to him on a daily basis, the one who chased away his no-good friends and poured away his liquor.

Tonight, she was almost subdued.

Tyrone felt unreasonable anger at the people around them. Couldn't they have been nicer to her?

More to the point... Couldn't *he* have been nicer to her?

Because while at the moment, the ladies and gentlemen of the *ton* were the ones judging her, the reason why she was being judged was Tyrone's fault.

Luckily, they were only a few paces away from his box. Soon, they'd be safely ensconced away from the prying eyes of the *ton*.

Before they were able to reach the box, an elegant woman stepped right in front of him, stopping him in his tracks.

Tyrone met the woman's eyes and anger rose up from inside him. Was she going to cause a scene in front of all these people?

He knew that she wasn't about to disappear just because he got married. She was no longer the mistress of his estates, but she was still a duchess.

The Dowager Duchess of Tyrone—his mother.

He smiled down at his wife. "Here we are. Do you mind going inside and waiting for me there?"

She glanced from him to the woman in front of them, and the confusion in her gaze was palpable. It was rude of him not to escort her inside and not to introduce his wife to his mother. He didn't care.

His mother was dead to him. And dead people didn't need introductions.

Pain flashed in his wife's eyes, telling Tyrone that she misinterpreted his behavior. She complied nonetheless, herding her family inside the box.

"Won't you introduce me to your bride?" his mother asked when they were left one on one.

"No." His answer was firm, succinct. Tyrone didn't want to give his mother a glimmer of hope.

"When I heard that you were at the theater," she continued softly, her gaze imploring, "I hoped we could share a box and—"

"No," he cut her off sharply.

She swallowed. "It is rather rude of you to interrupt me. Not to mention foregoing introducing me to your wife and her family."

Tyrone shrugged. "I wasn't taught manners at home."

She stiffened. "Xander—"

"It's Tyrone."

She lowered her eyes, her fingers playing with her reticule. "I hoped we could talk."

"And *I* hoped you'd come back for me... Twenty years ago. So I suppose we are both out of luck." He turned away, but his mother put her hand on his arm, stopping him.

And as much as he hated to admit that, her touch felt pleasant and comforting. Perhaps, she was a heartless woman. But she was also his mother. And his body knew that. Even his mind reverted to that little boy who once knew and loved her.

"You blame me for all the sins in the world," she said, her voice shaking. "And it's not fair."

"No." He swiveled back, shaking off her hand. "Just for one."

"I know that you're angry with me for leaving. I know you think that I abandoned you—"

"You did."

"I had to!" she cried, then looked around and swiped a lock of hair away from her face, her breathing labored. "You can't understand how difficult it is to be dependent upon a powerful man. A duke!"

"Can't I?" he barked. "I lived with him for two decades. I think I understand perfectly."

"It's different!" she insisted, her eyes filling with tears. "You were his son, his heir. And I was nothing."

"You were a duchess," he growled.

She let out a bitter chuckle. "And what is a duchess if not an accessory to a duke? I had no power, no leverage over him. I came to him with nothing. He could have starved me if he chose, and he did. He could have humiliated me in front of everyone, and he did. I had no recourse. He cut off my allowance and I had to beg him for scraps just so I wouldn't go barefoot."

Tyrone's gaze snapped to her face, his chest giving a sharp pang.

"Nothing in that house was mine," she continued, but he was barely listening. "The duchess's diamonds? They were only for show. They are entailed. I could not sell them. I could not pawn them. I had *nothing*. Not even you. Because you might have been my son, but you were his heir first and foremost. And he would never let you go."

A chill spread throughout Tyrone's limbs. But not because he felt sorry for his mother; he didn't. For the first time in a long time, he saw his own reflection and his father stared back at him.

I came to him with nothing. Just like his wife had.

He cut off my allowance... Just like Tyrone had.

He cleared his throat and nodded absently. "Thank you," he said and beheld his mother's surprised expression. "I thought that talking with you would be a waste of time. But while I was drinking my sorrows away, I forgot one thing I swore to never do."

"What's that?" she asked softly, reaching for him, hoping he'd take her hand.

"I promised to never turn into either of my parents." He turned away from her, banishing her from his mind.

He opened the curtain to the box, hoping to leave that conversation and his entire past behind.

～

Conversation buzzed around the box as the performance commenced.

It wasn't just their box. Hardly anyone was watching the show, making it difficult for Emily to concentrate. Not only that, but the duke seemed to be very tense as he sat beside her. He kept tapping his foot and nervously looking around. Sometimes he'd freeze as if he was figuring out a puzzle in his mind.

A few times he'd been addressed by one of the box occupants just to shrug the question away. Emily tried to pretend that she didn't care. Whatever he was going through, it was his problem and his problem alone. As to the identity of the woman they'd met before the show, Emily didn't need to know.

She was gorgeous, that woman. More gorgeous than Emily could aspire to be. And she'd commanded an air of elegance. Sure, she looked a bit older than Tyrone, but Emily could see her having young, rich, and powerful lovers. Like Tyrone.

She swallowed.

Her stomach churned, her heartbeat banging loudly in her ears.

Emily turned toward him and studied his frowning features. He bit his lip in concentration or consternation, as his knee jerked with every tap of his foot.

She gently placed her palm on his knee to stop his frantic movements. He turned toward her with such speed that she yanked her hand away.

He blinked at her as if woken from a dream, or rather a nightmare.

"I'm sorry," she whispered. "I didn't mean... You just looked troubled."

He shook his head, not in denial, but as if he was still not quite awake. Then he took a breath and looked around the box. The conversation was still flowing around them. Nobody seemed to pay any attention to them.

He turned to her and cracked a reassuring smile. "I was just lost in thought."

"About what?"

His smile turned easy as if he was about to make a jest or perhaps lie, but then he met her gaze and gave his head a little shake. "Honestly, I was thinking how I'd like to have a drink right now."

Emily's heart dropped right into her stomach. Did that woman have so much power over him as to drive him to drink again? "I really wish you wouldn't."

"Because you don't want me embarrassing you?" He didn't look at her as he asked the question.

Emily licked her lips then slowly, carefully, placed her hand on his jerking knee again, stilling his movements. This time he didn't jolt in surprise. He slowly turned his head, looking at her hand as if it were a foreign object he'd never seen before.

"No," she said softly. "Because I think I actually like you when you're sober."

He raised his brows. "You do?"

Emily smiled. "Well, the first time I saw you drunk, you nearly crushed me."

He snorted. "I saved your life."

"And the second time, you were entertained by a..." She paused and looked around. "I think you remember."

He let out a chuckle. "And you didn't like that?"

"Surprisingly, no," she answered with a smile.

"Do not worry. I am not about to start drinking. I know it

makes me an unlikable person. I know that it interferes with my rational thinking."

"Why do you drink then?"

He shrugged. "It's not the drinking that's alluring. It's just... it dulls the unwanted thoughts. It also washes this dull, gray existence with color. Makes everything more exciting for a moment."

Emily frowned. "And you never feel this way outside of drinking?"

He looked at her strangely, his eyes glinting with an unfathomable feeling. "Lately... Yes. More often than before."

Something in his tone of voice, in the look in his eyes, made Emily flush with heat. "You probably just need a distraction."

He nodded slowly. "Probably."

"Then what if I distracted you with something?"

He raised a brow suggestively, his next question coming quick and teasing. "In front of all these people?"

Emily couldn't help the chuckle that left her lips. One lift of the brow and she was already covered with a sheen of sweat, heat gathering low in her belly. She understood his implication. And yes, she would have loved to kiss him now to distract them both. She wished he would kiss her too, but not in an angry way as he'd kissed her before. But a real kiss. A gentle, passionate kiss. Her body trembled at the thought.

Emily briefly closed her eyes. She needed to return her mind to the present and help distract her husband. And she might as well get something out of it. Maybe, she could get to know her husband more, understand why he was the way he was. "What if you told me about yourself?" she offered.

He shifted uncomfortably in his seat. Emily moved to lift her hand off his knee, but he covered it with his, trapping her, causing warmth to flood her body. Then he looked her in the eyes. "What would you like to know?"

Surprised but glad that he was willing to entertain her questions, Emily perked up. "Anything. Everything. I do not know you at all aside from the things I learned through gossip."

"Gossip is not the most reliable source of information." One side of his mouth kicked up in a smile, his fingers lazily exploring hers. "You should know that more than anyone."

"I do." Emily smiled. Her heart raced, reacting to his subtle caresses. "So, tell me the non-gossip version of why they call you the Mad Duke?"

He laughed. "Pretty self-explanatory, don't you think?"

She shrugged. "Not really."

"You don't think I'm mad?" His fingers traced up her arm and then back again until he turned her hand palm up.

Emily laced her fingers with his, capturing him within her hold. "I've seen madder."

Her husband smiled. "Have you now?"

I've been madder. She wrinkled her nose remembering her unladylike behavior following their first meeting and up until they married... No, even after that. "I haven't witnessed you do anything mad." She scoffed as a certain picture came to her mind. "Except for whatever you were doing on the day we met."

He chuckled. "I was a lot madder when I was younger. I drank a lot, caused a lot of trouble, dueled over trivial things."

"What trivial things did you duel over?"

Tyrone resumed absently playing with her fingers. He did it easily, as if it was natural for him to do so, as if he'd done it thousands of times before. Emily found comfort in the action, until he said, "The honor of a dishonorable woman was the most common reason."

"Dishonorable?" She tensed.

"Yes. A married lady who spent her nights with me instead of her husband, for example. Or a young debutante who set her sights on trapping a duke."

Tyrone's fingers continued their lazy exploration of Emily's palm, tracing delicate circles and swirls that made her shiver. She held her breath, praying he wouldn't stop the intoxicating caresses.

"Trapping?" Emily finally managed, though his touch had scattered her thoughts.

"Mmhmm." His thumb stroked the sensitive skin of her inner wrist. "Tricking me into a compromising position."

Emily wet her suddenly dry lips. "Have... have many ladies tried to trap you?"

His lips quirked. "Some have tried. None have succeeded." His fingertips danced up the inside of her arm. "Until now."

A flush rose on Emily's cheeks. She met his heated gaze, heart pounding. "Have I trapped you then?"

"Completely." His hand slid around to cradle the nape of her neck. Emily swayed toward him, mouth parted in anticipation. "Somehow, I don't seem to mind."

His fingers tightened possessively, and then his mouth claimed hers in a searing kiss that stole Emily's breath. When at last he raised his head, her lips still throbbed from the pressure of his mouth and the caress of his tongue.

For a brief but passionate moment, she had forgotten that they weren't alone in the world. They were, in fact, in a crowded theater box filled with her family and her husband's friends. Her mother and siblings were sitting just a few seats away! And here she was unashamedly kissing her husband. For some odd reason, she couldn't force herself to care.

"Still think me less than mad, *mo tíogar*?" His rasping voice held a note of humor and something far more dangerous that thrilled her to her core.

Emily touched her swollen lips, shock and wonder and desire swirling through her. "Yes," she murmured. "For if you are mad, then I must be too."

Chapter Fifteen

A week had passed since their outing to the theater, and Emily was as confused as ever about the state of her marriage.

On one hand, the duke had become the most caring husband one could have ever asked for.

The day after the theater, he had invited Emily into his study and instructed his solicitor that he was now to work for Emily as well. He had dispensed Emily's allowance and opened credit in every major shop in London in her name. He had told her that he would pay for the governesses and tutors for her siblings from his own account.

He had also joined them for dinner every night since then. He wasn't very talkative, but a few remarks he made during conversations added levity, putting her siblings at ease.

He had even spent a portion of his time with Reggie, playing chess and showing him the stables, making Reggie light up with glee. He had suffered through her sisters' musical numbers without once showing his displeasure, and continued to show up to their lively evening entertainment as if there was nothing better he could do with his time. As if there was nothing else he would rather be doing.

He had teased Emily with words and seductive touches, and if looks could devour, she was certain she would not exist any longer.

Which made it even more perplexing that when the night fell, he was nowhere to be found.

Emily came to his bedchamber every evening to see if he desired to start their marital relations now that she had received her allowance, and also because she needed him to think the child she was carrying was his, but he was never in his room. She looked for him in his study, the library, and every other room of the house, hoping to run into him, speak with him, or sit with him in silence, steal a kiss or two, and maybe more, to no avail.

She didn't want to think where he spent his nights, but she couldn't help but lie awake all night wondering. And when he returned to his room in the early hours of the morning, he always locked his door as if afraid she was going to pounce on him and ravish him... Which was her ultimate goal.

She told herself that she *had* to do it. She had to seek him out. Not for pleasure, but for self-preservation and the future of her child. But the truth was, she just wanted to be near him. The world got warmer when he was near, whether it was from his body heat or the fire in his eyes.

Seeing him with her siblings, observing him more, she knew he would never hurt her child even if he found out the truth about her condition.

He would understand, she was certain. A person who was so gentle and patient with her and her siblings could never be the angry beast she used to think he was.

Yet she was too afraid to tell him the truth, nonetheless. Now that she'd experienced his warmth, she was afraid to lose it. If he knew that she'd tricked him into accepting another man's child as his heir, he would not be able to trust her.

And since there was no trust established between them to begin with, this would ruin any possibility of it in the future.

Emily had just crawled into the bed when she heard the door of the room next to hers open and close. And then the footsteps passed her door as Tyrone moved toward the stairs. Eager to finally find out where he went at night, Emily jumped out of bed and rushed to the door. Her stomach churned with anticipation but also fear. What if she didn't like the answer?

She peeked out of the door and caught a glimpse of Tyrone's cloak as he rounded the corner. Wrinkling her nose, she glanced at her bare feet before hastily scouring the room for her slippers and tugging them on.

She dashed out of the room, moving as quickly and as quietly as she could.

Her heart drummed violently in her chest as she followed him outside. He couldn't be leaving to see a mistress, could he? He was not coming to her bed... What was stopping him from visiting another's?

Emily wrapped her arms around her waist, shielding herself from the chilly wind and her ugly suspicions. He was headed for the stables. Of course, he was. He wasn't going to have an assignation in the back of the townhouse. Once he saddled a horse, how was Emily to follow him then?

She strangled a hysterical chuckle and hurried her steps. The only plan she had was to catch up to him and ask him all her questions. It was time.

When he disappeared inside the stables and everything went quiet, for a moment she worried that perhaps he did have a liaison planned. In the stables.

Emily silently slipped inside, listening to him cooing sweet words in the darkness. She stayed in the shadows, stepping lightly and making as little noise as she could—

Rip.

Her nightgown caught on a nail sticking out of the wooden

beam and ripped the fabric of her sleeve and the neckline, baring the upper left part of her body, including a bit of her breast.

Perfect!

She caught the fabric and tugged it up, mumbling something to herself when a pair of shiny hessian boots appeared before her eyes. So much for her stealthy approach. She raised her gaze to her husband's grim face.

"What are you doing here?" he bit out, holding a lantern over his head, a harsh light throwing shadows onto his face.

"I..." Emily wracked her brain to find an appropriate lie, but she came up blank. Finally, she blurted out the truth, "I am following you."

He blinked in stunned silence for a long moment. He probably didn't expect her to be upfront about her motives. Or perhaps he didn't expect *this* to be the motive. "Why are you following me?" He looked genuinely perplexed, and his gaze turned even more puzzled as he studied her from top to bottom.

She squirmed under his watchful eye. In her single, torn nightgown and flimsy slippers, she must have looked ridiculous and out of place in the stables on the cold spring night.

"To find out where you are going every night, obviously." She shrugged and collected more fabric in her fist to keep her gown from opening up. "Which I would still like to know. Including who you were talking to just now."

"How do you know that I am going out every night?" he asked as he hung the lantern on a nearby hook and proceeded to take off his cloak.

"Because—" *Because I come to your chamber every night hoping to start our marital relations.* Emily grimaced. She couldn't say that. No matter how upfront she wanted to be with her husband, that was just embarrassing. "I hear you leave your room every night. And I know you don't come back till the early hours of dawn. If you want to be secretive about it, you should be—" Emily paused her rambling as Tyrone stepped even closer, invading her space. He wrapped his arms around her before gently placing his cloak over her shoulders. "—quieter."

He tied the cloak at her neck and just stood there, refusing to vacate her personal space. "I wasn't trying to be secretive. I didn't think you'd care." He brushed a lock of hair away from her face. "And what are you doing not sleeping till the early hours of dawn?"

Emily took a deep breath, inhaling his comforting scent. He smelled of horses, soap, spice, and the hint of the outdoors.

And his heat had chased away her chills. He looked so powerful in a single shirt and buckskin breeches. Somehow larger than when he was dressed in formalwear.

"I read," she said. *And wait for you to come back.* "I don't get much time to myself during the day, so I take my time at night to relax and do what I enjoy in order to unwind."

"What keeps you so busy during the day?" His breath hit her cheek and her heart sped up, her stomach tumbling in an excited frenzy. His voice, his closeness played with her jittery mind.

"I... um... I have to find a governess and tutors for my siblings. And I need to buy them clothes. Now that I have my allowance, I have a lot of duties piled up that need taking care of, including this townhouse. It's been neglected for a long time."

"That does sound like a lot of work," he murmured.

"It is," she agreed.

"And so after a long day of working, searching for a governess and tutors, looking after your siblings, your mother, and the household, you relax by reading all night?" He raised a brow.

Emily let out a chuckle. "Yes. I need to redirect my thoughts. Otherwise, they take over and then I am not able to sleep at all."

She didn't expect him to understand. Her mind was too anxious to rest. She needed to keep it busy in order to quiet the thoughts in her head. Before, she'd always worried about stretching out the money just enough so her family wouldn't starve. She'd worried about teaching Reggie about running the estate when she didn't have enough knowledge herself. She'd worried about marrying off her sisters without dowries. Now, even though she was a duchess, most of those worries still persisted. And she had a few more added to her plate. How was she going to bring her husband's townhouse to its former glory? How was she going to get the approval of the *ton*? How was she going to tell her husband about the child that was growing inside her that was not his?

Was she ever going to build a closeness in their relationship that resembled the closeness her parents used to have or would they always have a gap between them?

To her surprise, he smirked and chucked her under her chin. "Who knew we had something in common?"

She blinked up at him. "Is that why you come here at night? You can't sleep either?"

He nodded. "The thoughts, the memories—they keep me awake. This place... this is the only place I have ever felt safe in this blasted house. So, I come here at night to regain a sense of calm. I talk to the horses." He chuckled. Emily looked past his shoulders to the stalls with the animals. She had to agree, this place felt quite cozy. "It doesn't always work. When it doesn't, I go for a ride."

Emily shivered under the great cloak and adjusted it over her shoulders. "Looking for an escape."

"Yes," he agreed. "Escape from this house. It is filled with memories that don't let my mind rest. That's why I started drinking myself into oblivion the moment I returned from the Continent. It dulled the pain and drowned out the echoes of the past. I can't sleep without a drink. Although it's not the drink that I want. I just don't want to be left one-on-one with my thoughts."

He stepped back and Emily instinctively reached for him. She grabbed his forearm and froze. *What am I doing?*

He froze as well, his gaze on her hand, watching it as if it was going to come to life and bite him.

She quickly removed her hand and nestled deeper into the cloak.

"You're cold." His frown deepened.

"No, I'm... Yes, a little."

He stepped closer once more and drew the edges of his cloak closer together. "We should go back to the house."

After what he'd just confessed, Emily didn't want to be the reason he was pulled back into the house that gave him so much grief. "You come out here so you're not alone with your thoughts and your memories."

He shrugged. "I suppose so."

She shook her head frantically. "I don't want to be the reason you're plagued with unpleasant thoughts tonight."

His warm fingers enveloped her cold ones, and he placed her hand in the crook of his elbow. "Something tells me that tonight will be an exception."

Chapter Sixteen

His wife shook, her teeth chattering slightly as they made their way back into the house. Her nose was rosy from the cold, her skin cool against his touch.

She was wearing a flimsy nightgown, old and threadbare, now ripped at the shoulder.

"Is your allowance not enough?" He couldn't help a rough note in his voice.

"Pardon?" She blinked up at him, a surprised expression in her eyes.

"Your allowance. It's been a week since I ordered my solicitor to dispense your allowance, is it not enough?"

"Why would you assume that?"

He waved a hand up and down in her general direction. "You're still wearing your old nightgown."

His duchess huddled further into his cloak. "I have ordered new clothing but it takes time for a modiste to sew them. Besides, I am not the only person in my family. My siblings come first, then my mother. And they have been humiliated enough. It is my job to look after them."

Something pinched inside Tyrone. Was it his heart? "Shouldn't your mother be the one to look after you?"

She looked at him as though he was daft. As if he didn't understand some universal truth. "She is ailing. A few days out of the month, she can't even leave her room. Besides, she raised me to my majority. Now it's my time to repay her for all she's done for me. I was the one who failed her. I should have married a long time ago."

Tyrone flinched. Despite his anger with the mothers of the world, he was the one who had failed his wife, not her mother.

He was her husband. It was his job to look after her now. Having never looked after anything in his entire life, and not having been looked after himself, he doubted he would be able to assume the role of husband very well.

Perhaps he should have thought twice about a decision made in his drunken haze to get married in order to keep his mother at bay. There were other more obvious and logical ways to dissuade her from approaching him. But logic was never at the forefront of his mind in his drunken state.

It was possible, however, that his mother wasn't the only reason he'd chosen to marry now—to marry *her*.

Maybe in the back of his mind, he'd known that he needed a tether, something tangible to get him out of his despair and apathy. Someone to help him claw his way from the coffin in which he'd locked himself together with the memories of his father.

Or perhaps, despite his protestations, he just didn't want to part with the woman who'd ignited a spark in his heart from the very first time they'd met. And his mother was just an excuse to do what he'd wanted to do in the first place.

Claim his wife as his.

Whatever his reasons, this woman now depended on him to be a reliable and competent husband. A duke.

She was strong and independent, and if he left his dukedom

and all his assets in her name, he was certain she would fare far better than he ever did.

There was a big enough load on her fragile shoulders, however, and something within Tyrone wanted to help her lift it.

They reached her room, and he ushered her inside, pausing at the threshold. He hadn't been in this room since the morning after their wedding. And he had a hard time recognizing it.

"Have you changed something here?"

Throwing a quick glance at their surroundings, she hurried toward the hearth. "Nothing significant. I have just moved the furniture around, placed some flowers, and replaced some pictures on the wall. Why?" Was that it? This room, like every other room in the house, used to fill him with dread. Perhaps, more so than other rooms. Now it felt warmer somehow—and it had nothing to do with the fact that they had just entered from the cold. It felt... cozier, brighter, more welcoming. Tyrone walked over to her bed, took the coverlet, and spread it before the fire. "Sit," he commanded as he took his cloak off her shoulders.

She complied and shifted closer to the fire, her hand still clutching the torn fabric at the shoulder.

"Do you have another nightgown?" he asked gruffly.

"I do. But I am too cold, I don't want to get it yet."

"I can—"

"Ow..." She hissed and moved her hand just enough for him to see a red scratch on her shoulder.

He frowned and knelt beside her. "Let me see."

She shook her head. "It's just a scratch."

Tyrone dismissed her words and brushed away her hands. He gently removed the fabric from her shoulder, letting it drop, revealing a view of her silky skin down to her breast. He didn't let his eyes wander, concentrating on the scratch, probably from the same nail that ripped her nightgown. The scratch was angry red, but it hadn't penetrated the skin.

He sat still, all his concentration going into not peeking lower at the tantalizing expanse of her skin.

"Is it that terrible?" She looked at him, a smile in her eyes. She was teasing him. And he still couldn't take his eyes off her.

"Not even a scar could ruin the perfection of your skin." His voice was low and hoarse. His entire body was taut, his breath shaky.

A glance at her bare shoulder was enough for him to start losing his mind. The sweet, floral scent of her perfume, mixed with the scent of her skin, only added to his confused state.

For one mad moment, he wanted to lower his head and lick her wound.

He moved to get up, but she stopped him with a hand on his shoulder. "Stay with me tonight."

She looked at him, her eyes vulnerable, beseeching him to stay. Women had used different techniques of seduction with him. Mostly, their flirtations were coy and playful. His wife, however, was direct. Calm. And somehow it aroused him even more.

"Do you know what you are saying?"

She nodded. "Yes. I am asking my husband to stay the night with me." She licked her lips, her cheeks turning crimson. The fire roared in the hearth, bathing the entire room in warm colors, heating Tyrone to the depths of his soul. "I am asking you to make me your wife... completely."

Tyrone didn't feel himself move. He was certain his wife didn't move either. Or perhaps they both did, at the same time. Somehow, their lips touched and then he was kissing her. And she was kissing him back. Feverishly. Passionately. Insistently.

Her hands locked behind his head, pulling him closer as she sipped on his lips, opening her mouth and slipping her tongue inside his.

Tyrone groaned and took over the kiss, plundering her mouth with an urgency he hadn't felt before. His body hardened, his chest, and his stomach burning from the inside and spreading the heat to the tips of his toes and fingers. He ran his hands down her shoulders, one bare, one still covered with the fabric of her nightgown. His fingers met just above her left breast, and he quickly ripped her gown in half.

She whimpered and gasped against his mouth, but instead of drawing away, she pressed her now bare breasts against his chest, her hardened nipples scratching against his shirt.

Oh, how he wished he didn't have his shirt on. He needed to feel her hands on his skin.

He tore his mouth away and tugged his shirt from his breeches before removing it over his head. There. Now he could enjoy—

Tyrone looked at his wife, and his breath caught. She was sitting on the floor—her legs curled to one side, her weight propped against one hand—completely naked, her torn nightgown pooling at her hips.

She was magnificent. The expanse of her milky-white skin invited his touch, and her dark pink nipples pointed at him, begging for his kiss. His gaze slid over her lovely rounded stomach, then the juncture between her legs, where the dark brown curls hid unknown delights. Unknown to him yet...

"Tyrone," she whispered, and he snapped his head to look at her.

"Don't call me that." His voice was hoarse, shaky.

She lowered her gaze, vulnerable and confused.

Cupping her cheek, he lifted her chin gently until she met his gaze. "I hate that name. Always have."

"Oh." She bit her lip, and he ran his thumb over it, freeing it from between her teeth. "What would you like me to call you then? Alexander?"

"No," he immediately said. Too close to what his mother used to call him.

She wrinkled her brows in thought, and he instantly smoothed them with his thumb. "Xander perhaps?"

He grimaced. "No."

"Master?" She raised her brow, a smile on her lips. "Your disgrace?"

Laughing, he dropped his hand, resting it on the floor next to her thigh. "You haven't called me that in a long time."

"You haven't been disgraceful in a long time." She chuckled. "My duke?"

Something caught in his chest. He liked the sound of that. It had nothing to do with the word duke, however. He just liked that she called him hers...

"How about... Alec?"

He looked at her, her sweet voice wafting around him pleasantly. Something about the way she called him Alec made him weak in the knees. "Yes. That'll do."

She smiled.

He took her hand and brought it to his lips. "And what would you like me to call you?"

She thought for a moment, then her eyes glinted with merriment. "Do you even know my name?"

He laughed and pressed a swift kiss on her lips. "I do... Emily."

Her smile gentled and her breaths came out more rapidly than before, her gaze darkening. "What about my last name?" she teased.

He faltered for a moment, not because he didn't know her name. He did. Only she wasn't Miss Emily Fitzwilliam anymore. His lips spread into a smile as she stared at him unblinking. "Blackwood," he said softly. "You're Emily Blackwood, the Duchess of Tyrone. My wife. *Mo tíogar.*" And then he kissed her.

Chapter Seventeen

E mily tasted like strawberries.

Her eyes fell closed, and a soft sigh left her lips as she returned his kiss with equal fervor. Her hands moved up his chest, leaving a scorching path in their wake. Wrapping her arms around his neck, she held onto him tightly and opened her mouth wider for his kiss, giving herself over to him completely.

He lay her gently onto the floor and continued devouring her sweet mouth. He roamed her body with his hands, not wanting to leave a single patch of skin untouched.

Her body responded to his every touch, lifting off the floor, pressing into his hand, demanding more contact. Soft sighs and moans left her parted lips as her head fell back, exposing her neck to his kisses.

Her skin tasted of sweet nectar, and her scent was almost magical, luring him closer to her, clouding his mind, and demanding release.

Every part of his body was taut with tension.

He wanted her like he had never wanted anything in his life. His cock pressed against his breeches, burning from the inside, begging to be free of the confining fabric.

Instead, he trailed his mouth down her chest over the slopes of her breasts.

"Alec, please!" Arching her back, she plunged her fingers into his hair and tugged. His name on her lips fanned the flames of his desire.

"Please, what?" He looked up at her as she squirmed beneath him. Her teeth nipped on her bottom lip, her gaze hazy.

"Please, kiss me," she whispered and brought his mouth over her hardened nipple.

He smiled before licking it.

He remembered the first time he ever saw her, buttoned up and oh-so-proper. He could never have imagined her begging for his kiss, pushing her breast into his mouth.

It made him all the more aroused. He opened his lips over her dark areola and sucked in her nipple as his hands explored her other breast, her perfectly rounded belly, and her well-shaped derriere.

Emily gasped, her back arching even more, her fingers tightening in his hair.

He flicked his tongue over her hardened peak, then sucked it in, before playing with it again, at the same time enjoying her passionate moans and the writhing of her body beneath him. She spread her knees and wrapped her legs around his thighs, pressing her hot and wet quim against the bulge in his breeches.

He hissed, wishing his cock was naked and covered in her arousal. He closed his eyes briefly, then moved to her other breast, performing the same ministrations as the tension rose from within him.

The scent of her desire enveloped him like a fog, and his mind refused to think of anything but her in his arms and the ways he could bring them both to pleasure.

With a growl, he slid down her body, trailing kisses as he moved.

She tugged on his hair, moving beneath him in agitation. "What are you doing?" she asked breathlessly.

He paused, his face directly over the mound between her legs, and licked his lips. He couldn't help the animalistic hunger that overtook him.

He kissed her belly right above the hairline and stared into her eyes. "I am making you my wife. In body and soul."

Confusion glinted in her eyes, and he smiled. No explanation would do it justice. He just had to show her.

So he lowered his head, spread her feminine lips with his fingers, and licked the seam. She shot off the floor and he had to hold her hips in place as he continued to lick her, lapping at her center, drinking her in.

God, he wanted more of her taste, more of the sounds that she made with every swipe of his tongue.

He moved his hands down her thighs, then gently anchored her knees over his shoulders to keep them both in place. Then his fingers went on exploring her stomach, the sweet globes of her breasts, his thumbs playing with her wet nipples.

She cried his name in between the sobs of pleasure, urging him on. He traced his tongue all over her sweet center, playing with the swollen, sensitive nub, circling it, discovering all the places that made her jump and tense.

She fell apart in his arms over and over again. But he quickly realized it took her only seconds of rest before she begged for his touch and his kiss again.

Insatiable minx.

He slipped a finger inside her hot, slick core and almost came from the feelings it evoked. Her muscles instinctively started drawing him in farther, her juices running down his hand. As his mouth continued sucking on her clitoris, he plunged a second finger and then a third inside her depth.

She cried out, her entire body tensing for what seemed like the thousandth time that night. Her inner muscles closed around his fingers, pulsating around him, drawing him farther inside. God, how he wanted to feel those pulsations with his cock. How he wanted to let her surround his cock and pull his orgasm with her own.

With a primal growl, he continued lapping at her quim until she stopped thrashing beneath him and lay limp on the floor, completely spent. Tyrone slowly withdrew his fingers and plopped onto his back beside her.

His cock was hard and swollen beneath his breeches, almost bursting from need. He covered it with his hand and squeezed. It took all of his willpower not to crawl on top of her and enter her in one quick thrust. It would have been so easy. She was so ready for him. Her arousal still dripped from his chin and covered his mouth.

He licked his lips and gathered her against his chest, burrowing his nose into her hair. "How do you feel?"

She let out a deep breath and answered with a weak smile. "Wonderful. Blissful." She paused. "Is this how a wife feels?"

He chuckled hoarsely. "*My* wife."

His body tensed against the pain in his cock, even as a feeling of peace washed over him.

He had never felt this sense of peace before. Not in the arms of any other woman. Especially not without having experienced his own orgasm.

His wife was full of surprises.

She looked up at him, and her eyes glinted with an unfathomable feeling. "I feel safe."

He swallowed and pressed a kiss to her forehead. He would never admit it to the tiny woman in his arms. But at that moment, with her in his arms, he felt safe, too. For the first time in a long time.

~

Emily lay in her husband's arms, filled with a sense of wonder. She had never thought she could ever feel this way. As if all the problems had disappeared and the entire world had fallen silent. As if there was nothing else in this world but her and him.

What he'd done to her just a moment ago was beyond shameful. She was not a virgin, far from it. She had experienced passion in another man's arms before as evidenced by the secret she harbored in her heart and in her belly. But what her husband made her feel over and over again with a flick of his tongue was something Emily had never imagined was possible.

And afterward, all the tension was drained from her body, leaving her limp but happy.

She turned in his arms, her fingers sifting through the soft, curly hairs on his hard chest. He was gorgeous, her rogue of a husband. She traced her finger down his body, enjoying every jump of his muscles in response to her touch. She explored his taut stomach, then followed the hair below his belly button down to his breeches.

She swallowed and glanced up at him. He was studying her features with a concentrated frown on his face.

Emily bit her lip. He'd seen her naked. Hell, he'd traced her body with his tongue! And she was yet to see him fully undressed. She was beyond curious and also, a tingle low in her belly danced every time she thought about his male organ.

She lowered her hand, her fingers struggling with the falls of his breeches.

Tyrone—no, Alec—chuckled and helped her undo them, before swiftly shedding and discarding the remainder of his clothes. When he lowered himself beside her once more, Emily could finally see his entire body illuminated in the warm glow of the fire.

He was... magnificent.

His thighs were hard and strong, betraying his love for horse riding. His stomach was flat, his chest and arms corded in muscles. But the most fascinating part of him stood proudly among the dark curls of hair, hard as steel but emanating inviting heat.

Emily circled her fingers around it, marveling at the soft skin over the hard steel-like rod. She ran her hand up and down the enticing length and Alec groaned. He covered her hand with his, gently guiding her, showing her what brought him pleasure. He squeezed his hand over hers, jerking and pumping his length.

Heat rose within Emily and soon she could not deny its call any longer. She straddled his thighs and used her second hand to explore his body, run her palm over his abdomen, and then lower to caress the sack between his legs. He jerked and his head fell back in pleasure.

Emily's belly squeezed and warmth seeped between her legs. Not only was it exciting to explore him, and touch him intimately, but it was arousing to see him receive pleasure from her touch. She wanted to bring him to the same bliss she'd experienced. She wanted to feel his body convulse beneath hers with pleasure.

Caressing his length, she brought her second hand over to his cock and ran her thumb over the glistening tip.

He hissed, his hips thrusting upward as he grabbed her by the elbows. His eyes, as dark as night, stared at her with animalistic need.

Emily couldn't take it anymore.

Placing her hands over his chest, she crawled over him and kissed him hungrily.

He responded with untamed ardor, his fingers plunging into her hair, drawing her closer. She could taste the salty essence of her own pleasure on his lips, his tongue, and somehow that aroused her even more. It reminded her of the things he had done to her and made her want more. Made her want to feel more of him.

"Please, Alec," she breathed, as her hips moved, rubbing her wet center over his hard and scorching cock, imploring him to enter her, to take her. "I want to feel you." *Inside.*

With a growl, Alec wrapped his arms around her and turned them over, pressing her against the rug on the floor, anchoring her with his weight. He kissed her deeply, hungrily, robbing her of any thought. As she caressed his tongue with hers, she could feel every little part of her that sensitively rubbed against his scorching skin.

She tensed, kneading his shoulders with her fingers as her muscles contracted and she felt emptiness in her center as she'd never felt before. Alec deepened the kiss, while his cock slid over her center, gathering her juices, gliding against her sensitive flesh. He thrust against her, teasing her swollen little nub with every move.

Emily could only moan and whimper, her hand on his hips, her fingers digging into his skin, encouraging him to move faster and faster, chasing the feeling of complete surrender, waiting for the pressure to build inside her before the ultimate release. With an untamed cry, she came apart in his arms again, lost in ecstasy.

He continued his thrusts for a few more moments before joining her in the blissful state.

His breathing loud and heavy, he collapsed on top of her, his weight comforting if a bit crushing.

He finally turned onto his side and playfully flicked her nipple.

"Ah! I'm still too sensitive," she squeaked with a chuckle and received a playful kiss in answer.

He rolled away, jumping to his feet and disappearing into the dressing room before reappearing again with a wet towel.

Emily was covered with sweat, but what she did not realize right away was that her husband's seed was on her belly.

He quickly cleaned up the juices between her legs and his own seed from her belly before discarding the towel. Then he took her into his arms, easily carrying her to the bed.

He helped her inside the covers and pressed a kiss to her forehead.

He hesitated for a moment, and a strange fear took place in the pit of her stomach. Was he going to leave?

Emily tugged on his arm, and it seemed to overpower whatever internal struggle he was having with himself. He quickly crawled into bed and gathered her against his chest.

The feeling of warmth and safety was slightly overshadowed by a nervousness in the pit of her stomach as he wrapped his arms around her. As pleasant—no, blissful, no... out of this world—as the experience had been for her, she knew that in order to sire a child, he needed to spill his seed inside of her, not on her belly. More importantly, she wanted to feel him inside. Not only his fingers and his tongue, but his engorged manhood. The single thought brought back the tingle low in her belly.

She knew it was wanton. *She* was wanton. But she couldn't help but feel rejected that he didn't feel the same.

A part of her, however, felt relief.

Because although it had been her goal to trick him into thinking that the child inside her was his, she didn't want that anymore.

Things had changed between them. She'd gotten to know her husband better. She'd come to care for him, and she thought he cared for her too, and for her family. He wasn't the man her mother feared him to be. And he deserved to know the truth about the child inside her.

It would've been better if she'd told him earlier, before they fell into each other's arms. Now she was afraid it would set their relationship back a step. He could withdraw his affection, grow distant from her. He might not want to share any more intimacies with her. Not just physical ones, but emotional ones, too. And he'd be within his right to do so.

But there could be no closeness between them when there was a large secret between them. She needed to tell him the truth.

Emily looked up at him, ready to do just that, only to see that his eyes were closed, his chest rising and falling with peaceful breaths.

He was asleep.

And a part of her was glad that she had a temporary reprieve.

Chapter Eighteen

Emily woke up in her bed alone.

The cold sheets on her husband's side let her know that he had left a long time ago, which was odd since the sun was just rising above the horizon. A fleeting memory of her waking up alone in bed each time Bernard had visited her crossed her mind. He used to climb up her window, spend a few hours, and climb back down before the night was over. It always left her feeling lonely, even rejected, although she understood the reasoning behind it.

Now that she was married, she'd thought she would never have to feel this way again. She had been wrong.

She longed to wake up in her husband's warm embrace. To feel as safe as she'd felt the night before.

Emily let out a deep sigh and rolled off the bed. She picked up the torn pieces of her shift and her cheeks burnt at the memory of her husband ripping the fabric and what came after.

She wanted to see him again. Did he want the same?

Did it matter?

She looked down at her belly and caressed it softly. It was

slightly rounded, but it wasn't obvious that a child rested within her womb.

Not yet.

She needed to tell her husband the truth before it became obvious. Before they reached further levels of intimacy. She needed to tell him now.

Having made up her mind, she made her way toward the dressing room to get clothed and brush out her hair. She glanced at the looking glass, at her short, wavy locks. She'd gotten used to her new hairstyle, she realized. She even liked it now.

She smiled, thinking of a little girl with short wavy hair just like hers and piercing green eyes just like Alec's. Emily bit on her inner cheek nervously and proceeded to get dressed.

The child she was carrying would not have Alec's eyes or anything of his. But the next one could.

They could be a real family. A large and happy family just like the one she had growing up. She had always wanted many children. Six or seven, perhaps.

Before she could dream of her happy future, she needed to talk to her husband and explain to him why she hadn't told him earlier.

Her husband, who was gentle, but also strong in spirit, would understand. He wouldn't fault her for doing what she did in order to save her family, she was certain.

Yet her palms still perspired and her limbs trembled, belying her conviction.

After all, Bernard, whom she'd known for years, had managed to betray her quite easily. And he was more steadfast, not as impulsive and passionate as her husband was.

Taking a deep breath, Emily smoothed the skirt of her day gown and walked toward the door.

Rap. Rap. Rap.

Emily started and let out a yelp as a maid opened the door.

"Your Grace, there's a modiste to see you. She insists she has an appointment."

Emily frowned. She had a couple of interviews with potential governesses lined up for her sisters, but they were in the afternoon. Before then, she had plenty of time to check on her mother, go over the estate details with Reggie, go over household issues with the housekeeper, and more importantly, talk to her husband. She was entirely certain she had no appointment with a modiste.

But as she made her way downstairs and met the woman who had arrived with two seamstresses, she realized that her husband was the one who arranged the appointment and insisted on having gowns and undergarments made for Emily with utmost haste.

She was rather annoyed but also oddly pleased with his heavy-handed approach to getting her new clothes.

She remembered his disapproving stare at her threadbare shift before tearing it in half the night before and smiled.

She would make certain to thank him for his generosity when she next saw him. In more ways than one.

The sense of calm that surrounded Tyrone when he was with his wife easily disappeared the moment he was one-on-one with his thoughts. As he perused his papers, his knee jerked with agitation, his fingers beating a staccato against the desk.

He had a lot of work.

He had abandoned his lands for months after his father's death. And although his managers were competent, things still had a way of falling apart. Everything needed constant control and control was something Tyrone had famously struggled with. Not only was he reminded of his own inadequacies on a daily basis trying to handle all the issues, but the moment he let his mind rest, the memories hounded him to the point that he needed to physically shake them off and force himself to concentrate.

At times, it worked. Other times, he needed to step away and join his newfound family in their daily activities just to squash his craving for liquor. Anything was preferable to the thoughts in his head that brought on tremors, sweating, and heart palpitations, even the less-than-perfect musical performances by his sisters-in-law.

Besides, it was worth it just for the chance to catch a glimpse of Emily as she watched her sisters like a proud mother hen, with a smile on her face and a gleam in her eyes.

More often than not, however, he found himself back in the study, confronting his own demons. He needed to learn everything he could about successfully running his estates if he were to teach Reggie to do the same.

The poor lad had an uphill battle when he turned of age, as his guardian seemed even more incompetent than Tyrone. For if Tyrone had resisted taking up his responsibility due to hatred toward his father and the memories that were about to swallow him whole, Reggie's guardian simply did not care.

It was unusual for Tyrone to care about someone other than himself. But when he looked at Reggie, he saw himself and wondered how he would have turned out if he had the support of his family. And then it made him want to give the little boy everything he had lacked as a child, including the encouragement, guidance, and support he wished he had gotten from his father.

Not to mention that it made Emily happy whenever he spent time with her family. And he was willing to do anything that made Emily happy. Her smile lit up the world, making it a cozy place to inhabit.

He turned the page of the document in front of him, coaxing his mind to concentrate when there was a timid knock at his door.

He cocked his head. Everyone to ever enter his study had used a more forceful knock to get his attention. Just as he thought that, the knocking intensified, getting louder.

"Come," he called and immediately stood as his wife entered the room. "Emily."

She smiled, her eyes glinting, the crests of her cheeks flushing. "I hope I am not interrupting."

"You are," he said softly and rounded the desk, approaching her with sure steps. "Thank God."

Her smile widened as she walked right into his embrace.

The next moment, his lips were on hers and just like that, without making a conscious decision, he was kissing her deeply, caressing her soft body as she melted into their passionate embrace.

Both of them were panting by the time they broke the kiss. She caressed his cheek tenderly, and he leaned into the warm touch.

"Thank you," she said with a twinkle in her eye.

He covered her hand with his. "You don't need to thank me for the kiss. I enjoyed it just as much as you did."

"No." She laughed, a beautiful musical sound that made his heart sing. "Not for that. For the clothes."

Tyrone disengaged her hand from his cheek and caressed her knuckles absently. "The clothes?"

"Yes, for commissioning a wardrobe for me and inviting a modiste into the house."

"Oh, that." He waved a careless hand. "I wonder why you didn't do it yourself."

"Because I don't want to waste your money. I could have waited for a couple of weeks and it would have been cheaper."

He pursed his lips. "Dear, you are a duchess. You need a wardrobe worthy of a duchess. I know you can walk around happily in rags as long as your family is clothed and go hungry for weeks as long as they are fed, but someone has to be looking out for you and..." He cleared his throat. "Since I am your husband, that someone should be me."

She averted her gaze, but her cheeks brightened in color. He took her both hands in his, caressing her fingers with his thumbs.

She wasn't wearing gloves, so he noticed a simple band on her ring finger. He brought her hand closer to study it. "Did I give you this ring?" He was ashamed he had to ask the question, but the truth was, he barely remembered their wedding day. And now that he thought about it, he should have given her a lot more jewelry. There were the duchess's jewels, of course, that she had access to. But that was old jewelry, tainted with bitter memories. She needed something new, something shinier. Something that would bring out her own brightness even more.

"No." She shook her head. "It is my mother's ring." She tugged it off her hand and brought it closer to his face. "It's engraved, see? It says Amelia. My mother's name. She gave it to me before you offered to marry me, when she thought we would be penniless, so that I could sell it. I kept it instead, and it came in handy when the minister asked if we had rings during our wedding, and you, well, hadn't."

Tyrone took the band and read the inscription on the inside. *Amelia.*

It was a simple silver band otherwise. Shame spread along his body and settled on the tips of his ears and his cheeks.

He hadn't even thought about getting a ring for the wedding ceremony. He cleared his throat. "It's... lovely." He handed the ring back, and she hesitated a moment before putting it back on.

She was so beautiful with her rosy cheeks, her bouncy locks, and inviting heat, not to mention her scent that lured him. He wanted to take her into his arms, place her on the desk, and devour her. His body came alive demanding completion.

The simple memory of her taste on his tongue almost made him come undone in his breeches. He let out a breath, calming his rioting mind.

He had already taken her once and finished on her belly without explaining why. He couldn't do it again.

Seeing how her eyes lit up every time she saw one of her siblings, he had an inkling that she wanted children of her own. Her own little family.

She would be an amazing mother, he knew. Not like the one he'd had.

Unfortunately, he would probably be a lot like his father. And he could not let that happen. But he couldn't keep deceiving her about his motives and taking her to his bed. If they were to continue their physical relationship, they should both be aware of the outcome.

"Emily—"

"Alec—" they said at the same time.

His stomach fluttered at the sound of his name on her lips. Both chuckled, and he waved a hand. "Please, proceed."

"No." She shook her head. "You first, please. I need to... um... collect my thoughts anyway."

"Very well." He squeezed her fingers. Not knowing how to gently ease into the subject, he blurted out, "I wanted to talk to you about children."

She whipped her head up, her eyes rounded, her mouth slightly open, shock evident on her features. "You did?"

"Yes." He stifled a grimace. "You see... I don't want them."

"You don't want children?" she asked on a breath.

"Yes. With the trajectory our relationship is taking, I can see a lot of nights and perhaps even days spent in your arms, and I just needed to tell you that those days and nights... they won't lead to a child. I want to be as honest with you as I can. And I know that I should have told you earlier, but I couldn't have anticipated coming to care about you and your wishes."

She tugged her hands out of his hold and took a step back, shaking her head. "This can't be. You are a duke. You need an heir."

He bit his lip. "I don't want an heir. I want my father's line to end with me and let my cousins or whoever else take over."

She stood speechless for a long moment before asking. "What does it mean for us? Will you never come to my bed again?"

A small smile tugged at his lips. "As you know from last night, there are other ways we can enjoy each other." When she didn't smile or even react to his answer, he continued, "We can be a real husband and wife. There are ways to prevent offspring. I've had numerous lovers and am yet to sire a bastard." He chuckled, but she didn't seem to appreciate his poor attempt to lighten the mood. "I am sorry. That was in bad taste. Are you... Will you be content without having children?" he finally asked, now interpreting her silence in a different way. Of course, she wanted a large family; she loved her numerous siblings. Would she resent him for trapping her in a childless marriage?

She licked her lips and looked straight into his eyes. "I am already with child."

His mind blank, Tyrone let out a chuckle of disbelief. "What we did last night, it wouldn't result in a child. And even if it did, you wouldn't be able to tell so quickly."

She shook her head and held his gaze. "Not yours."

His blood might as well have turned to ice inside his veins, so cold he felt. Frozen.

All the warmth and color sucked out of the room, he stood surrounded by the dreary silence. All he could hear was the ticking of the clock.

His mind refused to process the words, but in his heart, he already knew. She was the one who'd tricked him. She was the one who'd trapped him in this marriage for her own purposes. She was already with child when she came to beg him to marry her.

And then she'd tried to seduce him so she could pass her child as his own. Only now, knowing that her plan had failed, had she blurted out the truth.

All the thoughts still whirling around in his mind, wreaking havoc, he stalked toward the door. He needed to leave, clear his mind.

"Alec, please, don't go!" she called behind him.

His name on his lips still made her shiver. He paused, his hand on the doorknob, and said without turning to her, "It's Tyrone." Then he opened the door and walked away.

Chapter Nineteen

Tyrone stalked back and forth inside the walls of his bedchamber. The entire day he had tried his darndest to ignore his wife and his thoughts about her. He had pointed his mind in the direction of his work, then he had gone out on a late-night ride, but nothing had worked.

It was as if he was split in two pieces. One piece of him was angry at his duchess for her lie, admonishing himself for even daring to trust her because he'd known that women were trouble.

Another piece of him, however, screamed at him to go to his wife, to lose himself in her embrace. Now that he knew that she was already with child, they didn't have to restrain their passion.

But then he imagined her in the arms of another man, moaning beneath him, calling him to hold her tighter, kiss her harder—

Tyrone thrust his fingers into his hair and bit his lip to muffle the sounds of his agonized growl.

He wasn't being fair to her. He wasn't a virgin either. He had had numerous lovers. What did it matter if she had, too?

Because she'd lied to him about it. She came to him to beg

him to marry her, omitting a huge detail that would have changed everything.

She'd brought a cuckoo into his nest and expected to get away with it. If he hadn't told her about his conviction to not have a child, she might have never confessed at all. She would have led him to believe that the babe was his.

Legally, he could not do anything about it even if he tried. The child would be deemed his and he would have to accept it. Raise it. Be its father.

A painful knot originated in his stomach, his breathing accelerating.

He would be a terrible father; he knew it.

He was an undependable drunkard and a reprobate. Raising a child with him would be hell.

He almost wanted to fall to his knees before his wife and beg her for forgiveness in advance for what a terrible father he'd be.

But it was too late. Whether he wanted it or not, a child was coming.

And his pregnant wife sat in the room just behind the adjoining room's door, probably frightened and alone.

He stepped toward the door, an invisible cord tugging him to her.

She lied to me.

He turned away and stalked back to the hearth. His heart breaking, he knew that only she would be able to mend it. He glanced back at the door. He'd come to rely on her more than he'd thought.

If before, his first instinct was to reach for the bottle, now it was to look for her. Her gentle voice, that spark in her eyes, and the scent of her skin lured him to her side.

She made everything better with her simple presence.

His legs carried him toward her room. His hand landed on the doorknob—

She lied to me. On purpose. She tricked me.

He let go of the doorknob as if it scalded him and took two steps away when a knock sounded, causing him to whirl around.

He stared at the door in bewilderment as the knocking continued.

For all his struggle to stay away from her, he'd never imagined that *she* would come to him. Why would she? If she was a cold-hearted manipulator who'd tricked him into legitimizing her bastard child, her goal had been achieved. She didn't need him any longer.

And if she wasn't, she would be frightened.

There was no in-between in his mind. She was either scared of him or she didn't care for him at all.

And neither of those options would cause her to come to him in the middle of the night.

He slowly approached the door and opened it just as she raised her hand to knock once more.

"Oh," she said and lowered her arm.

She was wearing a billowing, silk dressing gown. A new dressing gown. The one he had urged the modiste to make for her only this morning. How she had managed it so quickly, he couldn't guess. Why was he fixating on a dressing gown?

Tyrone closed his eyes, yet he could still see his wife in his mind.

That's why. Because if he wasn't thinking about the inconsequential things, he'd have to think about her betrayal and trickery. Or about her welcoming heat, her soft, rosy lips, her inviting scent.

"Why are you here?" he asked roughly.

She stepped into the room, crowding him. "To apologize."

He scoffed and stalked away from her, suddenly cold and uncomfortable within his own skin.

"To explain."

"You don't need to explain," he said into the hearth. His fingers bit into the mantelpiece. "I understand perfectly. You were enjoying the wonders of the flesh before securing yourself a husband. You became with child, then took advantage of the scandal to rope me in as a husband." He turned to her, his eyes narrowed. "Or perhaps you orchestrated the entire thing. Created a scandal to trap me into marriage."

Her hands curled into fists by her side, and her chest rose with a deep breath, her nipples pressing against the thin fabric of her dressing gown. "Do you truly believe I would jump in front of a steam carriage in the hopes that you would be the one to catch me?"

He shrugged, crossing his arms over his chest. "Perhaps you didn't care exactly who was your savior."

"How would I even know that you'd be out on the street testing that abomination?" She waved a hand in frustration.

"Women have followed me around for weeks looking for an opportunity to catch me in a compromising position."

"I fail to understand why. If I were in a position to choose, you wouldn't be my first choice; you wouldn't even be the last!" She closed her eyes briefly, a grimace on her face, as she said it.

And although he understood the sentiment, he wished he could say it didn't hurt.

She hadn't wanted to marry him.

He could not really fault her for that. His own parents didn't want him, no wonder she didn't either. His only value lay with his title and money. And there were other men who could boast similar possessions.

"Who is the father?" he heard himself ask. *Why do I care?*

She swallowed. "Bernard. Viscount O'Malley's son. My former fiancé."

Tyrone knew the viscount but hadn't met his children. The viscount wasn't very memorable either. Average height, average build, average looks and intellect. Nothing that stood out about him. He wondered if his youngest son was superior in every way.

He must be, to catch Emily's eye.

"Does he know about the child?"

A pained grimace flashed across Emily's face. "I told him of my suspicions. But I wasn't certain then."

He nodded. "Now that we have this cleared out and you have secured yourself and your child a cozy future, you can get out of my room."

She stood motionless, her eyes on the floor, looking lost.

Tyrone had the urge to go to her, gather her in his arms, and comfort her.

He had to remind himself that she was a liar and a manipulator. So, he remained still.

"I am sorry that I hurt you," she finally said in a hoarse voice. "I was frightened and I had no choice but to do what I did. I regret the way it all unfolded, but I do not regret what it unfolded into. I came to care for you—"

He scoffed. "Cared for me so much you lied to me all this time?"

"Cared about you enough to tell you the truth!"

"*After* you got what you wanted. *After* realizing you wouldn't be able to trick me further!"

She opened her mouth to reply, but quickly closed it, proving his words to be true. She had planned to continue lying to him about the child. And that realization hurt more than he could bear.

"Get out."

"No." The obstinate woman shook her head. "I know I hurt you, but I also know that nights are difficult for you. I can't leave you alone. Especially not after an upsetting conversation."

He let out a hoarse laughter. "I don't need your pity."

"It's not about pity."

He prowled toward her, stopping less than a foot away. "What is it about then?"

"Compassion." Her liquid eyes stared right into his.

"I don't need that either."

She let out a frantic breath, fire brewing in those dark brown eyes of hers. "What do you want then?"

He looked her up and down. She was magnificent in her fury and desperation. His entire body went taut with just a glimpse of her. Now that he'd moved closer, he could smell the fragrant scent of her soap and her own essence.

What did he want? Her.

Beneath him. On top of him. Surrounding him.

To lose himself in her completely. To forget everything that had transpired between them. No. To forget everything.

Slowly, with a gentle touch of his fingers, he undid the sash of her dressing gown and held the edges apart, studying her form within. She was wearing a nightgown, but it was so flimsy as to be irrelevant. He could clearly make out the curvature of her body, the dark nipples, the patch of hair between her legs.

"You know what I want," he murmured.

Without a moment's hesitation, she slid her dressing gown off her shoulders. The nightgown followed, pooling at her feet, leaving her completely naked before him.

Gooseflesh covered her skin, and her breasts moved with her rapid breaths. His cock immediately grew hard, his heart drumming inside his chest.

"What are you doing?" he rasped.

She took a step, pressing her breasts to his chest. "What does it look like I am doing? I am doing what you want." With that, she stood on tiptoes and kissed his neck, the only exposed part of him she could reach. Her fingers reached for the top buttons of his shirt and started nimbly undoing them. Her mouth covered every inch of newly uncovered skin until there was nowhere to go. Then she tugged his shirt open and pressed her palms to his chest.

His heart accelerated, beating wildly against her hands.

Unwilling to let her see how much her touch rattled him, he commanded gruffly, "Undo my breeches."

Again, without skipping a beat, her hands settled on the falls of his breeches, her fingers shaking as she struggled to free him of the buttons.

Tyrone covered her hands with his. "Have you no pride?"

She looked up at him, her lips trembling, her eyes vulnerable. "Not everything is about pride, Alec. Some things are about caring for the people you l—" she shook her head. "—about comforting people you care about. Some things are about finding peace. Some things are about pleasure and passion."

He scoffed. "So, you will sell your pride for the price of what? My peace and comfort?"

"I am not selling anything. Pride has its time and place." She slowly undid all the buttons of his breeches, and let the fabric fall away. She tugged his shirt up, revealing his abdomen and his erect cock to her view. "Sometimes it needs to be shoved aside for other feelings to take charge. When I'm with you, pride is not at the forefront of my mind."

She slowly lowered herself to her knees and circled her fingers around his cock. She raised her eyes as her hand slowly glided up and down his length. "If you think you're degrading me or pressuring me into submission, you're not. I choose to submit to you. I want to."

She lowered her head and pressed a kiss to the top of his cock, then licked it and circled it with her tongue.

He groaned, his hand settling on her head, his fingers sifting through her hair.

"I want to spend the night with you as much as you do, perhaps even more," she said to his cock. "I want to explore your body and kiss you the way you kissed me last night. I want to find pleasure, bliss, and peace in your arms. So, why would I let pride get in the way of all the other feelings I possess?"

He didn't have an answer to that question. Or perhaps he did. But at that moment, his wife parted her lips and closed them around his cock. And all of his remaining thoughts disappeared from his mind.

Chapter Twenty

Seeing Emily naked, on her knees, with his cock between her lips, Tyrone let out a groan, his cock jumping from his overwhelming feelings.

She tentatively sucked on his tip, then raised her head and looked up at him.

"Tell me what to do," she whispered. "Teach me."

The words almost tumbled him over the edge. His fingers tightened in Emily's hair. "Take me in, *mo tíogar,*" he crooned. "Deeper. Yes. Just like that."

He guided her along his cock, gently tugging on her hair and letting go. His second hand curled around her fingers at the base, squeezing, pumping his length.

"Use your tongue," he whispered, and she immediately complied, soft whimpers leaving her throat as she gently explored his cock with her tongue, lips, and hands.

He continued urging her on, showing her exactly how to please him. She wasn't skilled at this type of lovemaking, it was obvious. But what she lacked in experience, she more than made up for in enthusiasm. Her moans and whimpers, the hunger in her eyes as she glanced up at him, taunted him, dared him to give in.

He could barely contain himself. All the sensations gathered in his cock, threatening to implode. He wanted to spill right into her mouth and as she licked the ridge of his cock, he almost did.

With a curse, he jerked away, taking a step back.

"No..." Emily whimpered, clutching his forearms.

He could sense her turmoil. She thought he was rejecting her. Not in a million years.

He helped her up and pulled her into an embrace. He kissed her shoulder, her neck, every bit of skin he could reach. She dropped her head back, giving him more access, and he took full advantage, sucking on her throat, lower down her chest, her breasts.

Swaying, she took a couple of steps back and he followed her blindly, until her back pressed against the wall. He sucked in her nipple, then opened his mouth wider, taking in more of her breast as his hands continued the exploration of her skin. She moaned, her back arching, then raised her knee.

Tyrone immediately hooked her leg over his arm and with one quick motion lifted her up, pressing her against the wall with his weight. He stared into her hazy, passion-filled gaze and smiled. He saw raw desire in her eyes, desire that rivaled his in its magnitude.

She might not love him. But she wanted him. And for tonight, that would do.

She plunged her fingers into his hair and kissed him wildly. Tyrone returned the kiss with full ardor, their desperate moans and the crackling of the fire the only sounds in the room. Without taking his mouth off her, he shifted to press his cock against her center. With one quick thrust, he seated himself inside her hot, wet depths. She broke off the kiss, staring into his eyes, her mouth slightly open, and moved.

His eyes fell closed, and he couldn't help the groan that left his lips.

She was so tight, so warm, and so damn beautiful.

"You feel so good," he rasped, then withdrew his length and thrust once more.

"Yes, Alec, please," she begged and he couldn't help but give in.

He thrust into her again and again with wild abandon, pressing her into the wall, rubbing his pelvis against her.

"Yes, yes, yes!" his wife cried, her arm stretched against the wall, her legs wrapped around his waist, her head thrown back in pure bliss.

He covered her mouth with his as she came, catching her cry of pleasure. She convulsed around him, tensing her body as her inner muscles pulsed, drawing his cock deeper and deeper inside, forcing him to follow her into the oblivion of ecstasy.

The next seven days followed a similar pattern. Emily woke up in her bed alone to find a leather rectangular box sitting on the pillow where her husband's head had rested the night before. The box contained a piece of jewelry. An expensive, magnificent piece of jewelry.

At first, Emily was elated to find the gifts, but the more days passed, the more it felt like a payment.

For the services rendered the night before.

Especially since beyond their nightly activities, her husband went out of his way to ignore her as much as he could.

He hid away in his study or spent the majority of the time out of the house. The only social gathering they'd attended, he'd escorted Emily and her mother into the ballroom, and then spent the entire evening in the card room with his friends.

And every time she attempted to speak to him when they were alone, he either distracted her with kisses or simply left the room and even the house.

The day of the Earl of Sutton's dinner wasn't any different. Her husband had disappeared early in the morning and Emily spent most of her day dealing with the household and entertaining visitors. During her free time, she had tea with her family and confided her troubles to her mother.

Emily knew she was at fault for tricking her husband. But she wished he would tell her what she could do to fix their relationship—or tell her anything at all.

When the time came for them to go to dinner, Emily was surprised to hear that her mother had retired early, citing a headache.

It wasn't uncommon for a migraine to strike out of nowhere, so she asked her sisters to take care of their mother and got ready for the outing.

Even though she felt bad for her mother's suffering, a part of her was a little glad that she had an opportunity to be stuck in an enclosed space—a carriage—with her husband, if for a short period of time.

Their next outing was the Gage ball in a week's time, and Emily was afraid her husband would hide in the card room during the entire event again. This was her only chance to have a tete-a-tete without distractions.

She wore her most elegant coral gown, with a low bodice that accentuated her breasts, which were fuller now as she progressed further into her pregnancy. She put a diamond choker on her neck and wore the bracelets her husband had gifted to her.

Her maid styled her hair into tight curls, and she finished her ensemble with a dark red fan.

She was quite happy with her appearance, so she wasn't surprised when her husband couldn't take his eyes off her from the moment he saw her, and even now, in the dimly lit carriage.

Her stomach tumbled and flipped inside her, her cheeks burning from his intense perusal.

"That gown looks marvelous on you," he murmured. Emily

held her breath, pleased that he was the one to start the conversation. Happier still that he'd started it with a compliment. Her happiness was short-lived, however, because he continued, "Who are you trying to impress? Sutton?"

"Sutton?" Emily repeated with genuine confusion. "Why would I want to impress another man?"

"Trying to find yourself a lover perhaps," he answered with a shrug. As if the idea didn't bother him one bit.

"And why would I need a lover when I have you?"

He scoffed.

Emily looked out the window, her fan tapping against her knee nervously, the hope for a civilized discourse dimming. "I resent your implication my morals are loose simply because I happened to share a bed with one man before I married you."

"How do I know it was just the one?" he asked roughly.

Emily snapped her head to meet his piercing green eyes. "And how many women have you shared your bed with?"

"It's not the same."

"Because you are a man?"

"No. Because I didn't bring another woman's offspring into our marriage."

Emily shook her head. "It is easy for you to judge me from your high throne. But if I gave birth to a child out of wedlock, I'd be shunned. My family would have suffered. Even if you were to bring another child into our lives, your standing in society wouldn't have changed."

"I understand that part, believe me." He leaned forward, resting his elbows on his knees. "I don't condemn you for making that choice. But forgive me for not trusting the loyalty of a woman who lied to me for weeks and tricked me into a marriage without disclosing the full truth."

"Because I feared for my safety!"

"I would never hurt you," he growled, his face getting closer to hers. Then he closed his eyes and leaned back against his seat.

Hiding in the shadows, he repeated slower now, calmer. "I would never hurt you."

"And I know that now. But you are judging me based on the actions of a woman who didn't know you at all. Once I did, I told you right away."

"You told me once you found out you wouldn't be able to pass your bastard as my child! Now that you're a duchess, I have no choice but to raise your bastard as my heir, give him my title, and—" He stopped abruptly.

"It's not like that! How many times—?"

"Actually." He raised a hand to halt her speech. "It's perfect."

"Do not interr—What?"

"It's perfect," he repeated quietly. "The reason I didn't want children was because I didn't want to leave my legacy behind. I wanted the Tyrone line to die with me, but this is more perfect!"

"What are you talking about?" Emily rubbed the bridge of her nose in confusion.

"Giving the title to someone not of my blood is ingenious! My father would be furious. It's the ultimate revenge." He settled back in his seat, crossing his arms over his chest. "I hope it's a boy."

Emily took a few moments to digest his words. "Is that really all there is to it?" she asked, bewildered. "Your actions were driven by your spite for someone who is dead?"

"He ruined my life," he said calmly. "I will ruin his legacy. It's only fair."

"No." She shook her head. "He ruined half of your life and you're letting him ruin the rest. Your pride is your poison, *Tyrone*." His burning gaze snapped to hers at the sound of his title. "It's killing you from the inside. Spiting your father doesn't hurt him. It's just hurting the people around you. People who are alive."

"I just came to terms with accepting your child as my heir," he said evenly. "Do you want me to reverse my decision?"

"I want you to make your decision based on something other than vengeance. You judged me because I was ruining your ultimate revenge on your deceased father. Now that you've figured out how this can further your revenge, all is suddenly forgiven. What if I give birth to a girl—"

"No. Everything is not forgiven," he interrupted her swiftly. "But you're a woman. I should have expected the lies and deceit."

"I beg your pardon!"

"I don't think I shall grant you the pardon."

"Do you really have such a low opinion of women? As if men are perfect!"

"No, of course not," he conceded easily. "I've obviously been disappointed by men, too. They are just... more direct. Women lie and cheat and sneak out in the middle of the night and leave their defenseless children alone and vulnerable."

"What?" Emily was getting vertigo from the way their conversation whipped around at every turn. Not to mention that her husband didn't seem to be listening to reason.

She didn't get any further elaboration, because at that moment the carriage came to a stop.

Alec helped her out of the carriage and they made their way inside the house, her body still trembling from the unsettling conversation.

They were welcomed into the house and escorted to the parlor where the guests were gathering. But the moment they stepped inside, Alec stopped short in his tracks.

Emily glanced from her husband to the small group of people in the parlor. She recognized a couple of men as his friends when Sutton approached them with a gorgeous woman on his arm. The woman they had seen before at the theater.

Alec's muscles tensed under Emily's fingers, his breaths quickened—he was like a cat, ready to pounce.

The earl stopped before them and sketched a bow. "Lovely to

see you here, Tyrone, Your Grace." He turned to his companion. "Your Grace, have you been introduced to your daughter-in-law?"

Emily's mouth opened wide as she looked from her husband to the woman before her. How had she not realized this before? The same green eyes, wide lips, and jet-black hair. Her husband was the spitting image of his mother.

The earl performed the introductions, as blood rushed into Emily's head, pounding loudly. But before she could say a word, Alec disengaged his arm and stepped away. "I've lost my appetite," he said, then turned on his heel and walked away, leaving Emily to stare after him.

Chapter Twenty-One

It took a long moment for Emily to realize that her husband had left her absolutely alone at his friend's dinner party. In front of his friends and his mother.

Tears pricked at the back of her eyes, and she had to press a hand to her stomach to regulate her breathing.

Sutton turned and waved someone over, before excusing himself and following Tyrone.

Lucien Drake stepped toward Emily and sketched a bow. "A pleasure to meet you again. Would you like to join our conversation?" She was certain he said something else, but she couldn't hear over the pounding in her head.

"Thank you. But I think I should follow my husband." She bobbed a curtsy and left the room.

Emily paused outside, her breathing accelerated, looking this way and that. Had Alec left the house? Was he hiding in one of the rooms on this floor? She slowly made her way toward the stairs as Sutton rounded the corridor.

"Duchess," he said, his breathing labored. "Let me escort you back into the parlor."

"Where is my husband?" She craned her neck to see if Alec

was behind Sutton. He wasn't.

The earl's face twisted. "He left. I apologize, it's my fault. I shouldn't have invited his mother without telling him in advance. But she asked for a chance to reconnect with her son, and I—" He grimaced. "Let us rejoin the other guests," he finished awkwardly.

Emily licked her dry lips. She glanced back at the empty corridor then returned her gaze to the earl, shaking her head. "I think I would like to go home."

He swallowed. "Of course. I shall have a carriage prepared for you. Would you like to wait in the parlor?"

Emily bit her lip to keep from crying, her face flushed in humiliation. Alec hadn't just left her to face an uncomfortable situation alone. He'd abandoned her.

She shook her head. She couldn't face all the people in there. Not now.

"I'd rather wait downstairs."

"Of course." Sutton offered his arm and together they made their way down in silence. He excused himself to call for a carriage while she collected her jacket and her gloves.

Light footsteps making their way down the grand staircase caught her attention. She turned to see the Dowager Duchess of Tyrone approaching her.

Emily froze, watching the woman elegantly glide down the stairs and traverse the hall before stopping a few steps away.

"Duchess," she said softly.

"Your Grace." Emily bobbed a quick curtsy.

The dowager stiffened, her hands briefly curled into fists before letting go. "I am glad to finally make your acquaintance. I've heard a lot about you."

Emily wished she could have said the same. "A pleasure."

"I wanted to apologize for the way we had to meet. I thought in a small company of friends, my son wouldn't be able to ignore me. Evidently, I was wrong."

"I haven't known him long," Emily admitted. "But I've come

to realize that he can ignore anyone under any circumstances if he puts his mind to it." She grimaced at the bitter tone of her voice. She wished she could control her emotions better.

"I have no doubt that his reaction hurt you, but I assure you that the fault lies with me, not you."

Emily swallowed. Perhaps the way he stormed away had nothing to do with Emily, but the fact that he left her behind spoke volumes against her.

"It is clear that he cares for you," the dowager continued, and Emily couldn't help the involuntary bitter laugh that left her lips.

"Is it?"

"And it is clear that you care for him, too." The dowager paused, wringing her hands. "I watched you that day at the theater. You couldn't take your eyes off each other."

Emily's breath caught. Oh, how humiliating, but that sweet memory washed gently over her bruised heart. Their quiet conversation, that gentle but scandalous kiss were their first steps toward a harmonious marriage. How fragile was their foundation to let that all crumble so easily?

A tear slid from the corner of her eye, and she wiped it away. "I do care for your son. But I don't know how much he cares for me if he didn't see fit to introduce me to his mother."

The dowager grimaced. "I assure you, it has nothing to do with you. He despises me."

Despises? Such a strong word. "Why?"

"He thinks I left him."

Emily frowned. *Women lie and cheat and sneak out in the middle of the night and leave their defenseless children alone and vulnerable.* "Left him?"

"Ran away from the house leaving him behind," the woman clarified.

"And you didn't?"

"I did." She looked down at her hands, fiddling with the skirt of her gown before meeting Emily's gaze again. "But I had no choice. You must understand. You are married to my son, a duke. You know how powerful one's husband is especially with a title such as his. Unlike my son, my husband was not a caring man. He was spiteful, angry, and violent to both me and my child. I tried to protect my son, but all I was left with were bruises and even broken ribs." She placed a hand against her stomach and took a deep breath before she was able to continue. "He wanted to get rid of me from the moment I gave birth to a son. And he didn't allow me to be close to my child, either. I stood in the way of 'disciplining' him. I was in the way of him becoming a man, a duke. I was simply in the way. If I hadn't run, I would have been dead. Not a minute goes by that I don't regret leaving my child with him. But if I hadn't, he would have tracked us down and he would have killed me. The duke didn't want me. But he wouldn't have stopped if I had taken his heir."

Emily's chest constricted. She was in a unique position to understand this woman's pain. That could have been her. If Alec was like his father, violent and angry, he could have killed her or her unborn child and nobody would have been able to intervene. Not even her family. But this poor woman in front of her didn't have a family it seemed. She had no one. Nothing.

But neither did her husband.

"How old was Alec?"

The dowager blinked up at her. "Pardon?"

"How old was your son when you left him?"

The duchess swallowed audibly, her chest rising with a heavy breath. "Nine. He was nine years old when I ran away."

Emily looked away.

"I left when I knew he would be safe at school for most of the year." She paused. "But I am back now. Although I realize that I cannot undo what I have done, I would love to form a relationship with my son. I would love to explain to him why I ran and how much I wish I hadn't. Even if it killed me."

"Do you truly wish you hadn't?" Emily asked.

The duchess licked her lips. "I would have probably been dead. But I would have the love of my child, so perhaps I do. I love seeing my son all grown up. But I wish I had been by his side while he was a child." Her eyes glistened, and Emily couldn't help but feel compassion for the woman who'd made an impossible choice. At the same time, she felt protective over her broken husband. The woman in front of her was partially responsible for his struggles, his nightmares.

"Why are you telling me this?"

The dowager clenched her fists. "I want to mend my relationship with my son. I don't expect you to beg him for forgiveness on my behalf. But perhaps you can arrange a meeting for us? One where he wouldn't escape. I am not asking for much, just for an opportunity to speak to him. To tell him my side."

The footsteps alerted Emily of someone's approach before the butler rounded the corner. "The carriage is ready, Your Grace."

Emily nodded and turned toward the dowager. "I can only promise that I will speak to my husband. But I can't promise he will listen to me."

The dowager nodded gratefully. "That's all I ask."

Emily found Alec in his room, sitting by the window, staring into the darkness. She tried to be silent in her approach, and he didn't give any indication that he'd noticed her until she was a few feet away.

"I apologize for leaving you behind," he said gravely.

"That wasn't nice," she agreed easily and stepped closer to him.

He let out a hoarse chuckle. "No, it wasn't. I am quite a bastard, aren't I?" Something glinted in his hand and Emily frowned.

"Sometimes," she said and took a few more steps until she saw his profile, his arm propped against his knee, a glass dangling from his fingers. Her gaze dropped lower to a bottle of whisky by the chair. "Where did you get that?" She pounced at him, her fingers closing over his hand.

He didn't protest, relinquishing the still-full glass of whisky. "Sutton's house."

With sure steps, Emily walked up to the hearth and emptied the glass into the fire. It hissed, the flames dancing brighter.

"Do not worry, I didn't even have a sip," he said from behind her.

Emily's hands shook. "You can't resort to drinking every time something unpleasant happens."

The chair creaked as he stood and walked toward her. "If I did it every time something unpleasant happened, I'd never have given it up."

She whirled around, her breath heavy, only to realize that he stood right behind her. She tipped her head back so she could look him in the eyes and swallowed. "Do you mean everything that has happened between us since our wedding has been unpleasant?"

He pursed his lips, his eyes roaming her face, then dropping to her lips before returning her gaze. "No, I suppose not."

They stood like that for a long moment, just inches apart, studying each other's features. His closeness was muddying her mind. She came to his room to talk about his mother, but now all she wanted was for him to kiss her.

He raised his finger and slowly, gently caressed her cheek, tucking a wayward lock of hair behind her ear as he did so. Emily swallowed. Her heart slammed against her ribs as heat spread along her limbs and low in her belly. She needed to speak up now or soon they would not be talking. "Why did you leave tonight?"

He grimaced, but instead of answering, he ran his finger down her neck, over her collarbone, then traced it along her bodice, over the tops of her breasts.

"Why haven't you told me about your mother?"

His eyes closed briefly before he slowly stepped to the side, his fingers still tracing along the bodice, then over her shoulder. Stepping behind her, he rubbed her neck. Emily caught her breath as he started undoing her gown.

"I gather that you don't want to talk, but—"

"I don't." He instantly cut her off.

"But I do."

The gown gave way and fell, pooling at her feet. Her stays followed, and she turned to him, her rumpled shift the only article of clothing clinging to her body. "Ale—"

He cut her off with a hungry kiss. His mouth slanted over hers, his hands roaming her body, pulling her closer to him. Emily couldn't help but return the kiss, her fingers clinging to his neck, drawing him even closer. His hands slid lower, squeezing her bottom, rubbing her belly over his hard length.

He wanted her.

She could feel it through his breeches, she could feel it in his ravaging kiss, in his possessive hands. And she wanted him, too.

But she wanted more than just physical closeness. She craved another kind of intimacy between them. The intimacy that she'd glimpsed for a brief moment before she told him about her condition.

She pulled away, a hand on his cheek, keeping him at bay and caressing him at the same time. "Alec..."

When he looked at her, his eyes were filled with pain. And Emily almost gave up her pursuit and just gave in to his demand. She wanted to comfort him with every fiber of her being. But giving in to passion just now seemed like the wrong kind of comfort.

"Why do you hate her so?" she whispered. She knew why from what his mother had told her. But she wanted to hear his version of events. His side of the story. "What has she done?"

With a groan, he pulled away, stalking toward the bed, then

back again. His eyes wild, he ran a hand through his hair, then clutched it. "Nothing," he finally said between his teeth. He dropped his hand and prowled away from her. "Absolutely nothing. When my father berated me for every little mistake, when he called me names and threw empty wine bottles at me, when he beat me for any perceived slight, do you know what she did? Absolutely nothing." He turned back, his gaze burning with fire, his voice crackling like a whip with every word. "And I still loved her. I curled up next to her when she cried, I hugged her whenever she was sad, I cried and yelled for him not to hurt her, although I was too small to make him stop. And did she do the same? No."

Emily's heart squeezed at the pain in his eyes. She imagined her husband as a little defenseless boy, under attack by a violent man twice his size—perhaps more—and nobody rushing to his side to protect him, to comfort him. And then her heart broke.

"No." She shook her head, refusing to believe a mother could have done that. There had been pain in the duchess's eyes. Perhaps, the duke kept the mother and son apart. "It was so long ago. How can you know that she didn't try to protect you? How do you know your memories are not warped?"

He smiled coldly, a smile Emily wished she'd never seen, a smile that sent shivers down her spine. "Because I remember quite clearly the morning I woke up and she was no longer there. I remember my father beating me, kicking me, telling me I was the reason she was gone. I remember crying myself to sleep begging for my mother to come back, to take me with her." He looked away, his gaze distant, an eerie calmness in his voice. "I had a trunk that I took to school every year. I collected all my belongings, packed them up, and stored the trunk by the window. Then I would climb atop the trunk and gaze out of the window, waiting for her to return. For me. But that day never came." He turned to her then, his features hard, and so was his voice. "So, you ask me what she did for me? Nothing. The only thing she ever did was for herself. She sold herself to a duke for the fortune and a title.

She gave him a son and once she'd had enough of my father and me, she left."

His gaze was full of anger and pain. His hands were fisted by his side, and his body coiled to jump at any moment. He was like an injured animal ready to attack. But unlike his mother, who had been afraid of her husband, Emily knew he'd never physically hurt her.

She walked up to him until she was only inches away and pressed a palm against his cheek. He twitched and looked at her with his questioning eyes. She framed his face with her palms and lowered his forehead to hers. "I am sorry," she whispered. "I am sorry for everything you've gone through."

He let out a breath, his shoulders slumping in relief. He circled his arms around her waist and drew her closer, his nose burrowing in the crook of her shoulder.

She ran soothing circles over his back and shoulders, wishing she could take his pain away. All this time, he'd lived with the firm belief that both his parents hated him. That nobody in the world loved him, and that he was worthless beyond his title. No wonder he was like a wounded animal. No wonder he resorted to drinking and vice. "I spoke to your mother today," she revealed quietly. He immediately tensed again. "And she told me that she was beaten every day. She told me he would have killed her if she didn't run, if she took you with her." He let out a scoff, but she continued, "How would you feel if she'd chosen to stay and then he'd killed her?"

He pulled away, enough to look her in the eyes. "I'd feel as though I was worth protecting."

"Would you?" She shook her head, rejecting his words. And at the same time, her heart broke from the conviction in his voice. "Because knowing you, I don't think you would. You'd feel guilt. You'd feel responsible for her death. You'd feel even worse than you feel today because she'd be dead. And you would not be able to tell her how it made you feel when she left you. Because she wouldn't be here. She would have left you forever. This way, she had an opportunity to come back to you."

He disengaged from her and took a step back. "You are defending her?"

"I am just offering another perspective."

He took another step back and raised a staying hand. "Tell me this, if your father had been an abusive jackal, if he hurt you, your sisters, and your little brother, but you the most. Would you have run away and left them behind? Left them with the angry despot who now had double the reasons to be ruthless?"

She swallowed. "I can't... I can't tell you that. I haven't been in that situation, and unless I had—"

"Well, let me tell *you*." He started pacing again. "You wouldn't. I know you. You came to me, a man you didn't know, a man you'd only heard ugly rumors about, to save your family. You sheltered them from me, poured all my whisky away, and faced my wrath, so I wouldn't frighten them. You did everything in your power to make certain the child you carry wouldn't end up a bastard. You would never leave your family behind. You would stay and protect them forever. Even if your own life was in danger."

Emily's stomach flipped inside her as her pulse quickened. Was there a note of forgiveness in his tone? He resented her for lying to him. He was hurt. But at least he understood why she did it.

"If my life was in danger..." She paused, taking a deep breath. "I don't know if I would have stayed. But I would have found a way to take them with me."

Alec nodded. "And that's the answer I knew you'd give me. And that's all I need to know about my mother."

"I am not saying that you should forgive her," she said quietly.

He paused and faced her fully. "What are you saying then?"

"I am saying that at least in this situation, you have the ability to talk to her. To ask her. To try and understand her. Not just for her sake. For yours. You've been carrying this anger toward her for so long, it almost crushed you. You can ignore her all you want after that. But you have an opportunity to find peace. If I were you... I'd take it."

Alec stepped toward her and grabbed her gently but firmly by the upper arms, his fingers caressing her skin. "I have already found my peace," he whispered hoarsely before planting a kiss on her lips. "Right here."

Chapter Twenty-Two

Tyrone didn't want to go to the Gage ball.

For one thing, he despised the man. The viscount had the ego of a duke, the reputation of a rake, and a complete disregard for society's rules. One might say he was exactly like Tyrone... except he had a loving family, including a wife he openly doted on—who was an actress by the way—talk about courting a scandal. Quite literally.

For another thing, Tyrone was certain that he would run into his mother again at that ball. And he wanted to avoid that at all costs.

But Emily was absolutely delighted at the idea of meeting Viscountess Gage, the actress and the owner of the Medusa theater, which was surprising considering the last time they went to the theater, she'd spent the entire performance facing away from the stage.

Still, she wanted to attend the ball, and he wasn't going to refuse her.

He loved seeing her bubble up in excitement and beam with joy. He would fight a storm without complaint if it brought a smile to her face.

He wanted to make her happy. So far, he'd been doing an extremely poor job of that.

He'd come to care for her in their short marriage. He loved her compassion for others, the care with which she approached everything she did, the way she'd befriended his staff and turned his residence into a home.

He couldn't help but admire the loyalty she had for the people she loved and her strength in the face of adversity. That was what had attracted him to her in the first place, even if he hadn't understood that at the time.

But seeing his mother at dinner the week before, he'd finally realized one thing. Emily hadn't known him when she married him. She thought him a reprobate and a rake, a drunkard and a violent man—all true in their own way. Still, she'd begged him to take her as his wife in order to save her family and protect her child. Then fought him every step of the way in order to ensure the safety and stability in her siblings' lives.

She'd entered a potentially dangerous situation for the rest of her life, knowing full well that she wouldn't be able to escape because so many people depended on her.

And that realization not only made him admire her more but also forgive her for the lie.

Perhaps, he wasn't as mad at her as he'd thought he was.

The thing that hurt was that he wished she loved him as much as she loved her family. Because if she did, then perhaps, with her by his side, he could take on the world.

But she didn't.

She'd only used him to benefit her family and her unborn child. And he was fine with that. As long as he could use her a little in return. Use her passion for their joint pleasure and her joy to bring him a semblance of peace.

They walked through the doors to the Gage ballroom, her hand in the crook of his arm, her hair bouncing with every step.

She was gorgeous, proudly looking out into the crowd of

people as the majordomo announced them as the Duke and the Duchess of Tyrone. They made their way downstairs and exchanged pleasantries with the hosts. The viscountess seemed genuinely pleased to make an acquaintance of the duchess. She quickly took her by the arm and led her away, citing the need to introduce her to her sisters-in-law.

Tyrone was loath to let go of his wife, but he had no choice but to acquiesce. He made awkward eye contact with Gage for one short moment after their wives left before turning away in search of acquaintances.

It wasn't hard. This ball was full of eccentrics, deviants, and otherwise scandalous individuals, a crowd of people Tyrone oddly felt comfortable around.

He made the rounds, talking with a few people, all the while not taking his gaze off his wife. She seemed to have found a group of women she felt comfortable with. Nobody dared to invite her to dance—clever men—and not a single man approached her without the company of his wife.

Tyrone relaxed, not quite certain why he was worried about other men approaching her in the first place.

He was so preoccupied with his wife that he didn't even notice the presence of another Duchess of Tyrone at the ball.

The only reason he noticed her at all was the hushed whispers from people around him.

And then he saw her approaching his wife. A smile. A friendly conversation.

Tyrone clenched his fists.

The mere sight of his mother made his chest hurt. He didn't need his wife making attempts to reunite them. He married her with the sole purpose of keeping the dowager at bay. And now she seemed to want to use his wife against him.

Emily hadn't spoken to him about the dowager since the night of the Sutton dinner. And he'd hope that would be the end of it. But his mother was a tenacious one. Perhaps, he needed to find out what she wanted from him. If she wanted money or jewelry, he was willing to give them to her if she agreed to disappear from his life.

Tyrone cut through the crowd with measured steps. He tried to regulate his breathing, thinking of the things he could say to her to keep the conversation short.

"You can have whatever you want," he'd say. "Enough money to leave the country and build yourself a small dowager estate off the British coast." Of course, that would probably not be enough. But he wouldn't be blackmailed into giving away his fortune. He'd earned it through his suffering. She hadn't.

What else could she want from him? Surely, nothing.

What if she was planning something with his wife? A double betrayal?

Tyrone expelled a breath. If he let himself, his thoughts would easily take him to dark places. He needed to avoid those places.

For a moment, people crossing the room blocked his view of his wife, and the next minute, she'd disappeared from his view. His mother did too.

Pausing his steps, he scanned the crowd and finally caught a glimpse of his wife exiting the ballroom with his mother in tow.

That didn't look good.

Whatever was going on, it was time for a confrontation.

Emily led the dowager away from the prying eyes. She'd agreed to have a short conversation with her. She owed her this much. But she refused to do it before the eyes of her distrusting husband.

They chatted about the weather and other inconsequential things on the way, but as soon as they stopped on the ground floor, under the grand staircase, the dowager asked, "How is your relationship with my son? He seems... content."

Emily clasped her hands together. She didn't know how to

answer that question honestly, and she wasn't certain she owed honesty to the woman before her regarding such an intimate subject. So, she answered simply, "It is as good as it can be."

The dowager smiled. "I am glad to hear that. The truth is, I was worried he wouldn't be able to make an agreeable match. And if he didn't, I'd feel it was my fault. For a long time, hearing about his debaucheries, I was even afraid he would turn out like his father. But he has goodness in him that flourished despite our failings."

"He is not a perfect man." Emily let out a chuckle. "Far from it, in fact. But I agree. His heart is pure."

The duchess glanced at her with a strange curiosity in her gaze. It seemed like she was about to ask a question, and Emily's stomach flipped in anticipation. But she shook her head, murmuring something to herself. When she faced Emily once more, there was a blank expression on her face.

"Could that possibly mean that I have a chance at mending my relationship with him as well?"

Emily cleared her throat and looked away uncomfortably. "I don't think he is ready for forgiveness. He has a lot of healing to do. I realize you're anxious to get to know your son better and to be part of his life. But you need to give him time and possibly space."

"We have lost so much time already," the dowager countered.

"Yes, because of your choices whether right or wrong. Now that you've shown yourself and made it known that you wish to see him, the choice to reconnect with you should be his." Seeing the duchess's pained expression, Emily added, "It hurts him to see you, I can tell. And I don't want him to hurt anymore."

A shuffle of approaching footsteps sounded above the staircase. Emily glanced upward but couldn't see anyone.

"Are you telling me to leave town?" the dowager asked.

"No." Emily shook her head. "It is not my place to demand that. What I am telling you is that it hurts him to see you. The rest, you can decide for yourself. If you do decide to leave, you can write him a letter expressing your thoughts and feelings and I shall pass it along to him. He can read it at his leisure and contact you when he's ready. That's as much as I can do for you. I have sympathy for you, I do, even if I can never understand your actions." Emily placed a protective hand over her belly. "I can't imagine what you lived through and I know you did what was necessary to survive. I wish I could help you get over the pain. But you're not my priority right now. My husband is."

The dowager smiled for the first time with a genuine smile although her eyes glistened with tears.

"I understand," she said softly. "And I am glad my son found a wife who loves him so deeply. Thank you."

Without waiting for Emily's reply, the dowager turned and walked toward the exit. She was leaving the ball. Good. It meant Alec didn't have to see her.

Emily let out a deep breath and slowly scaled the steps back to the first floor. She raised her head halfway up and noticed her husband standing on the landing, one hand gripping the banister.

Her cheeks heated, her stomach flipping in joy at the sight of him. "Alec, what are you doing here?"

He swallowed. "I was looking for you, actually."

Had he overheard her conversation with his mother? Her heart started racing faster. "What for?"

A quick frown graced his features before he relaxed. "I was hoping for a dance and then I noticed you weren't in the ballroom, so I came out to look for you."

A smile tugged at Emily's lips. "You looked for me just to ask me for a dance?"

He stepped closer. "Perhaps. Or perhaps I missed you."

He reached out his hand and Emily took it, her own hand shaking. His fingers closed around hers, enveloping her in familiar, calming heat.

"I missed you, too."

Chapter Twenty-Three

The dance with her husband was magical. This was the first time they'd danced together. And although it was a simple reel, she felt a closeness with him she'd never felt before. Something changed between them at that moment, and Emily wasn't quite sure what.

He looked at her differently. There was a twinkle in his smile that added a carefree boyishness to his rugged features. She loved to see that.

What she enjoyed more, however, was the fact that he didn't hide away in the card room after the dance. Instead, they walked around the ballroom together, engaging strangers in conversation. And through it all, he looked like a proud husband introducing his new wife into the world.

Halfway through the ball, a garter started feeling loose around her thigh and she excused herself to go to the retiring room.

She was flushed and slightly out of breath from spending hours in the crowded ballroom, so she spent a few minutes catching her breath.

The moment she walked back into the ballroom, Bernard stepped in front of her path.

Emily was so shocked to see him that for a moment she froze. The room spun slowly before her eyes, and she swayed on her feet. He immediately stepped toward her and grabbed her by the arm.

Emily wanted to yank her arm away, but a few people were already staring at them, and she didn't want to cause a scandal.

"What are you doing here, Bernard?" she asked, her voice suddenly breathless.

He offered his arm. "Would you allow me a short promenade around the room?"

Her first instinct was to say *no. Not in a million years. Not ever.*

A part of her, perhaps a foolish part of her, wished to know what he wanted to say. On the other hand, he'd never given her a chance to say her peace when she needed him.

"I believe that would be unwise," she said.

"Your refusal might lead to scandal."

"You must not have heard, but my tolerance for scandal has grown quite a bit since we last saw each other." Emily scanned the ballroom but couldn't see her husband anywhere. With her short stature, she was at a distinct disadvantage.

"I just need to say a few words," he pleaded.

"Then speak." Emily opened her fan and fluttered it lightly.

"We might be overheard."

"Then leave."

"Fine," he gritted through his teeth. "You always were obstinate."

"And you always were a coward," she retorted.

"You are too harsh, my darling."

"I am *not* your darling."

"But you could be again."

Emily, who was still scanning the crowd for a sign of her husband, snapped her eyes to her former betrothed. His deep blue eyes and his sandy-blond hair with a few curls were so familiar. Yet, nothing stirred inside her. "Whatever do you mean?"

"I've made a mistake, Emily. You must realize how difficult it was for me to hear about your betrayal. I couldn't think clearly for weeks."

"I have never betrayed you," Emily seethed. "Can you imagine how difficult it was for me to know the person I trusted the most abandoned me in my time of need because of gossip?"

"I didn't," he said, and reached for her hand, but Emily stepped back. She bumped her shoulder against someone passing them by, and they started attracting attention. *Blast.* She didn't need this. "My parents forced me to break things off with you," Bernard continued. "They forced me to start courting Miss Godfrey. And they refused to let me see you."

"They. They. They." Emily shook her head. "You're not a child, Bernard. You're capable of making your own decisions."

"But they threatened to disown me. At that moment I couldn't think of anything more terrible than that, but seeing you now, here, in the arms of another man... I can't imagine going through life without you."

Emily blinked, wondering whether it was appropriate to laugh. "That man is my husband. *I am married.* You do know that, correct?"

He stepped closer. This time, Emily assessed her surroundings before making a retreat.

"But the child inside you is mine, is it not? We're connected. Forever. I made a mistake. Have you never made one? Would you throw away a chance for us to be a family because of a simple mistake?"

Emily wondered if this was a dream and she was in the middle of a play to which she had not learned the lines. It seemed so nonsensical. "How?" was all she could muster.

"Run away with me." Bernard made another attempt to grab her hand and this time, he succeeded.

Emily twisted her arm away. She'd laugh if the entire exchange wasn't so disturbing. "I am married," she repeated, enunciating every word carefully.

"We can live in sin," Bernard continued, his eyes feverish. "We can go to France or Prague. Anywhere you want. Just the three of us. You, me, and the baby inside you."

Emily froze. *You would never leave your family behind. Even if your own life was in danger.* How could her husband know her so well after only being acquainted with her for a few weeks, yet the man who claimed to have loved her for years—the man *she* had thought she loved—knew so little? "If you truly think for a moment that I would even entertain your offer then you do not know me at all. And I do not know you either. But I thank you for finally opening my eyes. Although you broke my heart and shattered my trust, you are also the reason I married a man who knows what love and respect truly are. And I am immensely grateful to you for that."

A cruel, ugly laugh left his lips. "Tyrone? He wouldn't know respect if it knocked him over the head. He is a beast."

Emily's fingers curled into fists, her cheeks burning with anger. She hadn't known she would ever feel protective over her husband, especially since *she'd* thought him a beast just a few weeks prior. But she couldn't listen to this coward talk about her husband with such contempt in his voice. "He is more of a man than you will ever be. His name should never cross your vapid lips again."

"You used to enjoy my lips," he said with a twisted smile and Emily wondered how she had ever thought him handsome or kind.

"I didn't, Bernard. Until I married my husband, I simply didn't know what enjoyment truly was."

∾

"Tyrone?"

Tyrone turned to see Sutton standing before him. "Ah, Judas. Did you come to spring more family members on me?"

Sutton cleared his throat uncomfortably. He took out a cigar from his coat pocket. "I came to offer peace."

Tyrone nodded and both men stepped out on a balcony for a smoke. They stood in silence for a short moment, before Sutton said, "I only wanted what was best. I always thought you missed her."

Tyrone let out a cloud of smoke. "I did. But I would appreciate it if you let me deal with my own demons from now on."

"I vow not to engage in matchmaking of any kind from now on."

Tyrone looked at his friend and chuckled. "Occasionally you get it right," he said.

A small smile touched Sutton's lips. "I assume you're talking about your wife?"

Tyrone remembered overhearing his wife as she stood up for him against his mother, declaring him her priority, and he couldn't help but feel the warmth travel down his limbs. She was loyal and protective over the people she loved. Then perhaps it meant that—

Tyrone snuffed out his cigar and grinned. "If I were you, I'd quit while ahead." He tapped his friend on the shoulder and walked away.

When he entered the ballroom again, he immediately looked for his wife. This night, thus far, had been one of the best of his life. And he would have loved to continue it in the same way.

But his wife was nowhere to be found. She should have been back from the retiring room by now. Where was she?

He moved toward the exit, wondering if she was ill, or if something had happened to her, when he finally noticed her talking to a slim, blond man. At that exact moment, the man unceremoniously grabbed Emily's arm. Tyrone burned with anger at the oaf who dared such a liberty.

He was ready to tear the arms off the offender's body, but by the time he managed to reach his wife, pushing through the crowd, not only had she successfully shaken the man off, but he had slunk away, disappearing into the crowd.

"Who was that?" Tyrone barked. His demeanor changed as he noticed that Emily was pale and looked rather ill.

She immediately reached for him, and without thinking, Tyrone wrapped his arms around her.

He didn't care that they were in the middle of the ballroom or that dozens of disapproving matrons were going to whisper about them. His wife needed solace, and he would give it to her.

"What's wrong?" he whispered into her hair and pressed a kiss to the top of her head.

Emily took a deep breath, then leaned away from him, just enough to look him in the eye. "I just spoke to Bernard," she murmured weakly.

"Bernard?" Tyrone's entire body tensed. That dandy she was just talking to was her former fiancé? "Did he upset you?"

She nodded. "He did."

For a moment, all he could see was red. He wanted to find Bernard and rip his limbs off for upsetting his wife. One by one. But as the red cleared, he stared into his wife's vulnerable eyes. She needed him more. "What did he say?"

She looked him squarely in the eyes. "He asked me to run away with him."

All the insecurities within him screamed for him to ask her what she'd answered. A part of him wanted to inquire whether she'd agreed. But another part, not the jealous and insane part, the part that in the past few weeks had come to trust his wife and respect her, stayed calm. That same part of him prompted him to kiss her forehead. "Shall we go home, then?"

Her lips curled into a smile, illuminating the entire ballroom in the warm glow. "We shall."

Chapter Twenty-Four

The morning after the ball, Emily woke up in her bed, alone again, a solitary leather box lying on the pillow beside her. Last night had been like a magical tale. She'd danced with her husband, he'd held her in his arms in front of the crowded ball, and then they'd made love for hours when they got home.

But with the morning light, it seemed like nothing had changed.

Emily scrambled off the bed, wrapped a dressing gown over her nightgown, picked up the leather box, and flew into her husband's study.

Stopping a foot away from his desk, she asked, "What is this?"

Alec turned to his left and only then did Emily notice a man sitting there, taking notes. She covered herself tightly with the dressing gown, feeling quite foolish.

"You are free to go, Louis," Alec barked. He waited patiently while the man collected his papers and walked away.

When the door finally closed behind the poor man, Alec squinted at the box in Emily's hand. "I believe it's an emerald choker. You do not like emeralds. Is that it?"

He looked so serious, it took Emily all her strength not to laugh. "No, I am asking what does this mean?"

"It's a gift," he said simply.

"I realize that. But what for? For a night spent in my embrace?"

He frowned. "I don't understand."

"You keep me at arm's length. You come to me only at night or when you need a moment of pleasure and then reward me with these gifts." She threw the box onto the armchair. "I thought we made a step forward in our relationship."

He rubbed his forehead. "What are you talking about? Am I mistreating you in some way?"

"You're treating me like a mistress!"

Alec leaned against his chair, steepling his hands on his chest. "What would you know about being treated like a mistress?"

"I know that men spend their passion with a mistress, give her a shiny bauble, and then leave."

"Are you saying the jewelry I leave you is not worthy of a duchess?"

She frowned, more confused than before. "I am saying I do not want this jewelry!"

"What is it you want then?" he asked.

"I want you to treat me as your wife!"

He threw up his hands. "You are my wife!"

"Then treat me like one!"

He stood and rounded the desk, propping his hip on the edge. "My father beat his wife. I don't suppose you'd rather I treat you that way. My friend deposited his wife at his country seat and they haven't seen each other since the day they wed. Perhaps that would be more to your liking? I don't know any other way to be."

She paused in her indignation, staring at her husband in complete shock. How foolish could she be? Of course, he didn't know how to treat her. He'd never seen a respectful relationship between spouses. He didn't have a loving family like she did.

She swallowed and licked her lips, approaching him slowly. "What about a friend? How do you treat a friend?"

He scrubbed his face, his voice hoarse as he said, "Should we get drunk together and participate in debaucheries around town?"

Oh, her poor, poor husband. "Do you confide in them? Do you tell anyone your thoughts and share your burdens?"

"My solicitor." He waved a hand toward the closed door. "If the issues are truly serious, I'd employ his expertise."

Emily couldn't help but grimace. No wonder he avoided her at all costs. His instinct was to bury his feelings since he had never shared them with anyone.

Perhaps he did when he was drinking with his friends. Now that he had given that up, there was no safe place for him to do that.

She stepped between his knees and took his hands in hers, squeezing his fingers. "How about I tell you my vision of our married life and you tell me whether that's something you would like to have. And please, feel free to tell me if it's not. I won't be offended."

He nodded. "Very well."

"I want to wake up next to you every morning because seeing you first thing after I wake up would bring me joy. I want to spend evenings in the parlor, playing games, or in the music room, singing songs, or doing some other family activity and I want to be by your side because I enjoy your company. Every night before bed, I want to have long conversations about how our day went, discussing hurdles either of us encountered, and giving each other advice and encouragement. Or perhaps talking about literature, gossip, and the news. I want to be able to tell you anything that bothers me, receive support from you, and give you support when you need it. I want to be the first person you come to when you receive good news or bad, when you are happy or sad, when there's a problem you can't solve, or when you want to see me just because. I want you to seek me out during the day and not hide away in this dank room. I want to see you. I want to talk with you. Dance with you. Make love with you. Be around you."

He looked at her with eyes full of vulnerability. "I don't think I know how to do any of that."

She smiled and rose on her tiptoes until she was able to brush a kiss on his lips. His arms immediately closed around her waist, like they always did when she reached for him. "I think you're already doing it."

He tightened his arms around her. "I am serious. Do you think I do not want to see you during the day? That's all I want. But I am afraid to say something harsh. I am afraid to hurt your feelings. I am terrified of doing something wrong and pushing you away. I might be a gentleman, but I am not a gentle man."

Emily shook her head. "You are wrong."

"I don't know how to be a husband," he continued. "But more importantly, what terrifies me even more is that I know for certain that I will be an abominable father to your child."

"Impossible."

"I am barely able to be an adequate duke. Add more responsibilities and I shall crumble."

She placed her hands on his chest, feeling his panicked heartbeat. "Is this truly how you see yourself?"

"Did you not just burst through these doors to tell me I am a poor excuse for a husband?" One side of his mouth kicked up in a sad smile.

Emily pursed her lips to keep herself from laughing, her eyes glinting with mirth. "No, I burst in here to tell you that you can be better." She let out a breath. "I am not going to tell you that you are a perfect gentleman or an excellent husband."

"Thank you," he said dryly, "Now I feel a lot better."

"What I am going to tell you, however," she continued, ignoring his sarcastic remark, "is that I believe you can be."

He raised a brow. "Why would you believe in me when no one else has?"

Her heart constricted in her chest, her throat tightening. She had to swallow before she could speak. "Perhaps I see something in you that no one else has."

He covered her hands with his. "What is it you see?"

"The real you. The man who saved me when no one else would. The man who stopped drinking when no one thought he could. The man who stepped up to his responsibility as a duke even when it hurt. A man with great strength, resolve, and honor."

"You're describing someone else." He shook his head.

"And yet I'm not. You have all those qualities and more. And you might have needed a nudge, but you did all the work yourself and after seeing that, how can I not believe in you?"

"Because you also saw me at my lowest—avoiding my responsibilities and drinking myself into oblivion. Being rude and disrespectful."

Emily licked her lips, curling her fingers into his shirt. "I would never judge a man solely on his mistakes. Everyone makes mistakes. It's what we do after that counts and determines what kind of people we are. God knows I've made my share or do you think I am perfect? The woman who got with child out of wedlock and tricked another man into marrying her? Do you think I don't get up some mornings and feel like I've already lost and there's no point to anything in this life? I do. More than you know." She pressed a palm to his cheek. "Some days I feel so defeated that I even fail to do the basic chores. But I wake up the next day and try again. So, yes, I know you will make more mistakes, it is inevitable. You will not be a perfect husband, a perfect parent, or a perfect human every day. But as long as you wake up the next day and the day after and try again, you cannot fail."

Alec sat there silent for a few long minutes, and Emily waited for him to sift through his thoughts in peace. She stood between his knees, caressing his upper arms gently.

Finally, he raised his hand and slowly, tenderly pressed it against her belly. "Then I think it is time for us to go home."

Emily's eyes widened as she struggled to comprehend his words.

"To Ireland," he clarified. "Before it's too difficult for you to travel. I want to show you our home. My country seat. I want our first child to be born there."

Warmth spread from the place he was touching her throughout her body to the tips of her toes and fingers.

Our first child.

She leaned forward and kissed him on the lips. "I would like that very much."

～

Alec had promised his wife to try to be the best version of himself he could possibly be. And he wasn't certain what he was about to do next qualified. Or if he was falling back on his bad habits. All he knew was that it needed to be done.

He left the house in the afternoon, and now stood in a dark parlor, awaiting an audience. The door opened, and a slim, short man—perhaps, just compared to Alec—with blond hair entered the room.

"Your Grace." The man sketched a bow, freezing only a few steps away from the door.

"No need to ask for refreshments, O'Malley," Alec said. "I shan't be long."

Bernard swallowed, his Adam's apple bobbing nervously. "To what do I owe the pleasure?"

Alec walked toward him with measured steps. To his surprise, the shorter man didn't back away.

"You know who I am, do you not?" Alec raised a brow.

Bernard nodded. "The Duke of Tyrone, of course."

Alec tsked and shook his head. "I am not talking about the respectable Duke of Tyrone right now. I am talking about the Mad Duke. The one who races like a devil, drinks like a sailor, and wins duels even when deep in his cups."

Bernard cocked his head but remained silent.

"Well, if you come too close to my wife ever again," Alec said hoarsely, "you'll know the sharp end of my sword."

Bernard let out a nervous chuckle. "Surely, you are not mad enough to duel over your wife's honor. It would besmirch her reputation."

"They call me the Mad Duke for a reason, O'Malley. I care not one whit about a reputation. I care about you staying away from my wife."

Bernard's lips twisted in an ugly smile. "As it happens, I do know you, Mad Duke. The man who can't stay sober for more than a day. A man who abandoned his dukedom to rot. A feral man who duels at the sound of a sneeze. You brought disgrace to your name. You've been sober for two days and suddenly you think you're a better man than I am? What makes you think you can suddenly become the husband she deserves?"

Alec smirked lightly. A few days ago, hearing this would've triggered his temper. It would've prompted him to hit the bastard in the face causing disgrace to his name once more. Proving to the world that he was still the same Mad Duke as before. But now, it only made him smile. "Because *she* believes I can." He passed Bernard and paused at the door. "She also believes that you're a piece of horse crap. And she is always right."

Chapter Twenty-Five

Ireland
Two months later...

"You can open your eyes now." A violent drumming of her heart followed the command.

Emily nearly burst from anticipation. Alec had brought her into the nursery but insisted she close her eyes before stepping inside. Now, as she opened them, she had to blink a couple of times to get used to the light, and then her mouth slacked open in awe.

She twirled around the room taking in the new decor. The previously dull white walls now shone a crisp sky blue, with a border of playful angels dancing across the ceiling. The newly made furniture, toys, and a full wall lined with books and puzzles adorned the room.

When she'd seen this room the first time she arrived at the estate, she'd been horrified. Now it looked like the most cheerful room in the house.

"It's beautiful!" she breathed, taking in every little detail. "I think I want to live here."

Alec chuckled and shook his head. "Then I'd have to move here, too. You know I can't sleep without you."

Emily rose on tiptoes in an attempt to kiss his chin. But he dipped his head and caught her lips. Kissing her deeply, his arms immediately wrapped around her, holding her close.

"Thank you," Emily whispered against his lips. "I never dreamed it would be ready so quickly."

He shrugged. "I told you, we shall renovate the entire estate before the little one's arrival."

Emily let out a giggle, sincerely amused by the idea.

"I have one more surprise for you today," he said against her hair. Emily felt him shiver against her body. Was he nervous or simply cold?

She raised her eyes and saw uncertainty in his. Wanting to dispel the tension, she asked, "How many more surprises should I be expecting?"

His smile gentled. "In a lifetime or a day?"

Now it was Emily's turn to be nervous. Despite his teasing tone, something about the look in his eyes told her that he had been waiting for this moment for a long time.

He dipped his hand into the inner pocket of his coat and fished something out. With shaking fingers, he extended a silver ring toward her. "I never gave you a wedding ring."

Emily held her breath as she picked up a gorgeous silver ring with a depiction of two hands clasping a heart surmounted by a crown.

"It's a traditional Irish Claddagh ring," he explained. "It signifies commitment between two people. The hands symbolize friendship, the crown symbolizes loyalty, and the heart..."

"Symbolizes love," Emily finished for him. Twisting it in her hands, she noticed an inscription along the inside. "*Mo tíogar,*" she read aloud, and a huge smile spread across her face.

Gripping her hand tightly in his, Alec leaned his forehead against hers.

"Thank you," Emily whispered.

He shook his head. "No, *mo tíogar*, thank you. I don't know what I would be without you. I was going into a downward spiral. You saved me."

Her smile gentled. "You saved me first."

Alec took the ring from her hands and slipped it onto her left ring finger, a heart pointing toward her. Still holding her hand in his, he murmured, "With this ring, I thee wed. With my body, I thee worship. With all my worldly goods, I thee endow." He swiped a lock of hair away from her face. "I promise to love you and keep you safe from the day I met you till the last beating of my heart."

"From the day you met me?" She chuckled, although the tears burned at the back of her eyes.

"Exactly. I love you. And have loved you from the moment I laid my eyes on you. It just took me a while to figure it out."

She stood on her tiptoes and pressed a kiss to his lips. "I love you, too—Ah!"

She reared back, and he grabbed her by the arms, his eyes comically large.

"Is anything amiss?"

"No!" She clasped his hand and pressed it against her rounded belly. "Do you feel it?"

He stared at her for a silent moment, then she felt a small but distinct twitch in her belly again.

"Is that—?"

"It is!" Emily laughed, and Alec wrapped his arms around her before twirling her in glee.

"Our little one is finally saying hello."

Emily smiled. "I think he is saying he likes his room."

Alec smiled, although there was still a hint of fear in his eyes. Emily could not fault him for that. She was frightened as well. Moving to Ireland where the memories of his childhood haunted

Alec at every corner, having their first child, all those experiences were new and frightening. But as long as they were together, they could face it all.

Epilogue

Alec prowled inside his room like a wild beast, tugging on his hair, wishing he could have been with his wife.

A birthing chamber was not a room for men. At least, not until the babe was born.

Emily's loud screams tore his heart apart, and the only thing that kept him from barging in and holding her was that breaking the door would cause more turmoil for his wife. The midwife had already locked the door against him so he wouldn't keep distracting them.

Then everything went quiet, and he leaned against the door, listening for any little sound, wondering if everything was fine.

The door opened then and Mrs. Fitzwilliam appeared on the other side with a wide smile on her face. "Please, come in."

Before she finished the sentence, Alec was already by Emily's bed.

He took her hand and pressed a kiss to her temple, then his gaze fell to a tiny bundle in her arms.

He swallowed, studying the odd-looking, rosy, wrinkled creature. It was so tiny, and not at all what he imagined babies looked like, although, he wasn't certain exactly what he'd imagined, either.

"Are you all right?" he asked his wife, and she nodded with a smile.

"Tired. But yes, we are well." She raised the babe slightly in her arms, a questioning gaze in her eyes. "Do you want to hold her?"

"Her?" Alec's voice broke a little, and he had to clear his throat. For a moment, all his fears of inadequacy flashed in his mind.

"Yes." Emily's smile widened as he took his daughter into his arms.

She was so very tiny, so fragile. His fears disappeared and only love, gentleness, and protectiveness overtook his heart.

"Welcome to the world," Alec said, unable to take his eyes off the little miracle in his arms. "You don't have to worry about anything, *mo tíogarín*, Papa will keep you safe."

The End.

Keep reading for a special preview of Book Four in The Rake Review, *It's Raining Rakes in April* by Annabelle Anders!

Enjoyed the book? More are to come. Sutton, Lucien Drake, and even Chaos are slated to get their stories. Sign-up to my newsletter to receive new release updates!

http://sendfox.com/sadiebosque

Oh and as a bonus you'll get a prequel Christmas novella *How the Scot Stole Christmas* completely free! (and other perks!)

To find more of my books browse my website:
www.sadiebosque.com

Coming Soon

Book 4 in The Rake Review, *It's Raining Rakes in April* by Annabelle Anders.

An undercover duke and a clumsy, but ambitious, debutante

Everyone knows debutantes will do anything to marry a duke, which is precisely why this season, the Duke of Ridgefield is going undercover as yet another notorious rake—the mysterious Mr. Pope.

As the eldest of seven sisters, Miss Julia Rigsby has one task in life—marry well. The trouble is, she's clueless when it comes to flirting.

Might she learn a trick or two from one of London's handsome, rakes? Mr. Pope, it seems, might make for a capable teacher, not to mention, easy on the eyes...

~

CHAPTER 1

Hyde Park, April 3rd of 1820

Dearest Readers,

With Easter behind us, the Season is underway, which means the marriage mart is well and truly open! One question begs answering: will proper courting and successful matches take center stage, or will those proper unions be overshadowed by the inevitable titillating scandals? Mayfair abounds with debutantes to be certain, but will these gentle ladies parse out the reprehensible rogues from gentlemen with honorable intentions?

A conundrum, truly, because what lady can resist a rakish fellow? Denying oneself is the ultimate test of decorum and restraint, is it not?

Of other import, nearly seven years have passed since the Duke of R-s death and the heir apparent has yet to return to claim his title, and if he's declared deceased, Mr. Phillip Birdwhistle will become a most eligible bachelor, indeed. A duke may be on the market, ladies! And a young and wealthy one at that!

    Unless Lord Arthur William Henri Lepope returns to claim his dukedom, and I am pleased to share that I have heard whispers of just that. Even so, having been away from our genteel kingdom for so long, he may very well be uncivilized and corrupt.

    Regardless, this Season promises to be a most interesting one. And this author, without question, will be watching it all.

    Until next month,

    The Brazen Belle

Henri Pope skimmed the ridiculous article and then carefully folded it into a small sailboat. After examining its seaworthiness, he then crouched at the bank of the Serpentine, set it in the water and gave it a gentle push, smirking as it sailed away. No doubt, members of the *ton* would consider him uncivilized—he was also cynical, disillusioned, and perhaps a little depraved.

Even so, he wasn't about to become some simpering gel's treasure chest.

Henri stared across the water, rippling from a gust of wind that carried the promise of rain. The small craft, however, held steady, and Henri experienced an absurd pang of jealousy. Or perhaps not so absurd—because his days of sailing were over.

The second pang wasn't jealousy at all, but sadness.

His older brother has passed nearly seven years earlier, but the news hadn't reached him until this past winter—in the form of a pleading letter from his mother.

"Your brother perished in an accident—racing to Brighton. Come home," she'd begged. *"I pray my message finds you before your cousin has you declared dead. He is all but salivating at the prospect of becoming Ridgefield."*

Henri glanced over his shoulder to where Phillip Birdwhistle languished amidst a flurry of feminine attention. Dressed in turquoise velvet from a comically tall top hat to his padded calves, Henri's cousin was bound for tremendous disappointment.

Because Henri was not, in fact, dead.

Just as he turned back to watch his little ship sail away, a nervous-looking lady caught his attention. She was watching Phillip and his admirers from where she stood on the Serpentine shoreline. Gray eyes, fringed with thick lashes, narrowed, and her nose scrunched up. She looked the picture of a person gathering their courage right as they were about to do something quite foolish.

Obviously yet another young woman hedging her bets in the hopes of landing a duke. She stole a glance at the water behind her, and then back to the small group not ten feet away.

Curious as to how this chit intended to gain his cousin's attention, Henri made himself comfortable on the slightly damp ground. He plucked a sliver of grass and chewed on it, prepared to be entertained.

And was not at all disappointed.

The girl, dressed in pale pink muslin and lace was of average height, and even as he watched she tripped over...

Nothing.

When she shot the offending section of lawn a disapproving scowl, and then impatiently shoved the flaps of her bonnet back, Henri chuckled silently. The obnoxious hat not only covered her head, but flopped around her face, allowing brief glimpses of her features, which from what he could see were... average as well.

As though coming to a decision, she turned in Henri's direction, removed a handkerchief from her bodice, and then very deliberately dropped it at the water's edge.

Henri's gaze lingered on her bodice. Although her gown was modestly cut, the snug bodice provided more than a generous view of delightful cleavage.

Perhaps she wasn't as average as he'd first believed.

Moving the blade of grass to the opposite side of his mouth, Henri unapologetically watched Miss Pink and Perky glide along the shore—or attempt to glide—since this particular miss lacked the grace required to *truly* glide.

The chit snuck a backwards look and, unnoticed, stomped back to retrieve the white scrap of linen. Henri's laughter was lost in a rumble of thunder, punctuated by another gust of wind.

He'd have to return to his townhouse soon, but first he'd see how the charade before him played out.

The desperate lady fisted her hands on her waist even as a flurry of manufactured giggles rose from around Phillip. Henri recognized the amusement as contrived, having learned such tricks the hard way.

In a manner that ensured he would never fall for such schemes again. That had been too painful.

Moreover, he would not be tricked into making an offer to a woman he didn't care for, or even worse—manipulated into a situation where he inadvertently compromised some simpering child.

Flutters of lace drew his gaze to Miss Pink and Perky again. The wind was picking up, and the effect of her gown pressed against her front shouldn't have affected him as much as it did.

Pursing her lips, she crouched low and then burst up, tossing the handkerchief over her head. And this time, it hung in the air while she pretended to stroll away. Hopefully this poor young woman didn't hold any aspirations to take to the stage. Because the ploy was as obvious as he'd ever seen.

That handkerchief might as well have been an untethered kite. Henri couldn't help but grin as he watched it float over the water. When had he last felt so lighthearted? Perhaps he should thank her.

Because her efforts were... the worst he'd ever seen, and for the first time in weeks, he wasn't feeling pulled down by his own circumstances.

One of Phillip's pastel-covered admirers noticed the ploy, but Henri's cousin remained oblivious. But of course, why would he when there was a petite, blue-eyed blonde grasping his arm, almost child-like in her apparent innocence.

Henri propped his hands in the grass behind him and leaned back, crossing his ankles as the few last remnants of sunshine warmed his well-worn Hessians and tan breeches.

Having been away from England for nearly seven years, Henri wasn't at all concerned that someone would recognize him. While attending Cambridge, he'd grown taller than all the other boys. The taller he'd grown, the skinnier he'd looked, and bullies had labeled him a beanpole, teasing him relentlessly.

A few of those bullies had taken the teasing beyond words, taking every opportunity presented to humiliate Henri, the second son of a duke. Tk had graduated a decade earlier, so he'd been left to fend for himself.

It hadn't helped that he'd been forced to dress to the nines, with his hair slicked back, or that he'd been cursed with sparse peach fuzz along his jaw and over his upper lip until after he'd reached his majority.

Henri raised a hand to his unshaven chin and stroked the coarse hairs. He was quite certain he wouldn't be recognized.

Loath as he was to dwell on the past, Henri dragged his attention back to the chit wearing pink. She was frowning at something in the water.

Ah yes, the handkerchief. Nearly ten feet away from shore it appeared to be slowly sinking.

She glanced back towards Phillip and then out to the water again.

Henri assessed her possibilities. True, a few medium sized rocks could possibly function as steps, but they wouldn't be stable and, most likely, were covered in moss.

But time was running out. The handkerchief was saturated now. It would be on the bottom of the river very quickly.

She hitched her skirts, revealing stocking-covered ankles, and reached one foot forward, and then another. This was not going to end well.

Oh hell.

"Stop!" Henri called out.

It's Raining Rakes in April will be available on April 1, 2024 and is now available for pre-order.

Mad Duke: The Inspiration

The Mad Duke was inspired by a real-life figure, Henry Beresford, the Marquess of Waterford, better known as the Mad Marquess.

Waterford, just like the hero of my book, was famous for his numerous pranks, excessive drinking, and his contempt for women.

I made a few nods to the original historical figure in the book, once even calling the hero the Mad Marquess.

Some sources suggest that Waterford was the reason for coining the term "Paint the town red." Unlike our hero, who ruined a lady in an attempt to save her from the steam carriage, Waterford and his companions painted a tollhouse, the constables, and a good portion of the street with red paint after refusing to pay at the Thorpe End tollgate in an inebriated state.

Like our hero, he was also an avid horseman. He similarly retired to his estate in Ireland and reportedly lived an exemplary life after getting married.

Historical Note

Barley seeds as a pregnancy test

In this book, we see Emily confirm her suspicions of pregnancy by examining sprouted barley seeds. It is implied, although I didn't go into details, that the seeds were soaked in urine for a few nights, and the fact that they grew indicated that she was indeed pregnant. While this method of diagnosing pregnancy was not popular during Regency times, it was actually a much older method used by Ancient Egyptians, Greco-Romans, and also in Russia during the 17th and 18th centuries. So it is safe to assume that not trusting Tyrone's doctor to be discreet, Emily read about this method in one of her books and decided to try it out.

The most surprising thing about this method, however, is its accuracy. Scientists have tested this method during modern times and found about an 80-85% accuracy rate. (Note: Not much is known about these studies, including the test sample. The effectiveness of this method can also vary due to factors such as environmental conditions, seed quality, and individual interpretation. However, I think it's reliable enough for a fictional story.) It was more accurate with a positive result, i.e., when a woman was pregnant, than with a negative result. So the fact that this method had worked for Emily is not surprising.

If you're interested in learning more about the history of pregnancy tests, check out this fun educational video on <u>Youtube</u>.

Also by Sadie Bosque

Made in the USA
Coppell, TX
22 March 2024

30448453R00127